Praise for the work of *USA TODAY* bestselling author Jennifer Greene

"A book by Jennifer Greene hums with an unbeatable combination of sexual chemistry and heartwarming emotion."
—*New York Times* bestselling author Susan Elizabeth Phillips

"A spellbinding storyteller of uncommon brilliance, the fabulous Jennifer Greene is one of the romance genre's greatest gifts to the world of popular fiction."
—*Romantic Times*

"Jennifer Greene's writing possesses a modern sensibility and frankness that is vivid, fresh, and often funny."
—*Publishers Weekly* on *The Woman Most Likely To*

"Combining expertly craft characters with lovely prose flavored with sassy wit, Greene constructs a superb tale of love lost and found, dreams discarded and rediscovered, and the importance of family and friendship…"
—*Booklist* on *Where Is He Now?*

"Ms. Greene lavishes her talents on every book she writes."
—*Rendezvous*

Dear Reader,

Welcome to another fabulous month of novels from Silhouette Desire. Our DYNASTIES: THE ASHTONS continuity continues with Kristi Gold's *Mistaken for a Mistress*. Ford Ashton sets out to find the truth about who really murdered his grandfather and believes the answers may lie with the man's mistress—but who is Kerry Roarke *really?* *USA TODAY* bestselling author Jennifer Greene is back with a stellar novel, *Hot to the Touch*. You'll love this wounded veteran hero and the feisty female whose special touch heals him.

TEXAS CATTLEMAN'S CLUB: THE SECRET DIARY presents its second installment with *Less-than-Innocent Invitation* by Shirley Rogers. It seems this millionaire rancher has to keep tabs on his ex-girlfriend by putting her up at his Texas spread. Oh, poor girl...trapped with a sexy—wealthy—cowboy! There's a brand-new KING OF HEARTS book by Katherine Garbera as the mysterious El Rey's matchmaking attempts continue in *Rock Me All Night*. Linda Conrad begins a compelling new miniseries called THE GYPSY INHERITANCE, the first of which is *Seduction by the Book*. Look for the remaining two novels to follow in September and October. And finally, Laura Wright winds up her royal series with *Her Royal Bed*. There's lots of revenge, royalty and romance to be enjoyed.

Thanks for choosing Silhouette Desire. In the coming months be sure to look for titles by authors Peggy Moreland, Annette Broadrick and the incomparable Diana Palmer.

Happy reading!

Melissa Jeglinski

Melissa Jeglinski
Senior Editor
Silhouette Desire

Please address questions and book requests to:
Silhouette Reader Service
U.S.: 3010 Walden Ave., P.O. Box 1325, Buffalo, NY 14269
Canadian: P.O. Box 609, Fort Erie, Ont. L2A 5X3

Hot to the Touch

JENNIFER GREENE

Published by Silhouette Books
America's Publisher of Contemporary Romance

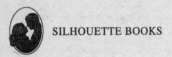 **SILHOUETTE BOOKS**

ISBN 0-373-76670-X

HOT TO THE TOUCH

This edition published by arrangement with Harlequin Books S.A.

® and TM are trademarks of Harlequin Books S.A., used under license. Trademarks indicated with ® are registered in the United States Patent and Trade Mark Office, the Canadian Trade Marks Office and in other countries.

Visit Silhouette Books at www.eHarlequin.com

Printed in U.S.A.

Books by Jennifer Greene

Silhouette Desire

Body and Soul #263
Foolish Pleasure #293
Madam's Room #326
Dear Reader #350
Minx #366
Lady Be Good #385
Love Potion #421
The Castle Keep #439
Lady of the Island #463
Night of the Hunter #481
Dancing in the Dark #498
Heat Wave #553
Slow Dance #600
Night Light #619
Falconer #671
Just Like Old Times #728
It Had To Be You #756
Quicksand #786
*Bewitched #847
*Bothered #855
*Bewildered #861
A Groom for Red Riding Hood #893
Single Dad #931
Arizona Heat #966
†The Unwilling Bride #998
†Bachelor Mom #1046
Nobody's Princess #1087
A Baby in His In-Box #1129
Her Holiday Secret #1178
The Honor Bound Groom #1190
**Prince Charming's Child #1225
**Kiss Your Prince Charming #1245
§Rock Solid #1316
Millionaire M.D. #1340
††Wild in the Field #1545
††Wild in the Mooonlight #1588
††Wild in the Moment #1622
Hot to the Touch #1670

Silhouette Intimate Moments

Secrets #221
Devil's Night #305
Broken Blossom #345
Pink Topaz #418

Silhouette Special Edition

•†The 200% Wife #1111

Silhouette Books

Birds, Bees and Babies 1990
"Riley's Baby"

Santa's Little Helpers 1995
"Twelfth Night"

Fortune's Children
The Baby Chase

Gifts of Fortune
"The Christmas House"

Harlequin NEXT

Lucky #2

*Jock's Boys
†The Stanford Sisters
§Body & Soul
**Happily Ever After
††The Scent of Lavender

JENNIFER GREENE

lives near Lake Michigan with her husband and two children. Before writing full-time, she worked as a teacher and a personnel manager. Michigan State University honored her as an "outstanding woman graduate" for her work with women on campus.

Ms. Greene has written more than fifty category romances, for which she has won numerous awards, including two RITA® Awards from the Romance Writers of America in the Best Short Contemporary Books category, and a Career Achievement Award from *Romantic Times* magazine.

One

Respect was a touchy issue for Phoebe Schneider. She'd been a skilled physical therapist for several years, and since no one had twisted her arm and forced her to become a masseuse, it was pretty crazy to complain. Maybe a lot of guys assumed that being a masseuse meant she was loose as a goose, but guys, by their hormonal nature, always indulged in wishful thinking.

At twenty-eight, Phoebe knew perfectly well how the world worked. She just had a little hot spot about the respect thing…say, the size of a mountain.

Today, though, was one of those rare, fabulous days when Phoebe felt so great about her job that any price she had to pay was worth it.

From the windows of the Gold River Hospital conference room, the Smokies loomed in the distance. The mountains were still shawled in snow, the wind still February sharp, but inside, the temperature was toasty. The pediatrics neurologist, pediatrics head and ICU nurse rubbed elbows at the table. Phoebe wasn't just the youngest of the group, but distinctly the only masseuse.

What tickled her pride bone most, though, was that they were all listening to her. Of course, they'd better—because when the subject was babies, Phoebe was known to fight down and dirty.

"We've been through this before. The problem," she said firmly, "is that you're all looking for an illness. A pathology. Some kind of disease you can fix. But when you've ruled out all those possibilities, you have to look at other choices." She clicked her mouse, which changed the screen image on the far wall to that of a three-month-old baby. "George isn't sick. George is cold."

"Cold—" Dr. Reynolds started to interrupt.

"I meant emotionally cold." She clicked the mouse again, showing a picture from the day the baby had been brought into the hospital. A nurse was lifting George from a crib. The baby was indistinguishable from an inanimate doll, because his little arms and legs were as rigid as stone. "You already know his history. Found in a closet, half-starved. A birth mother incapable of mothering or even basic care. This was simply a baby who was born into a world so hostile that he had no concept of emotional connection."

She showed the next series of slides, illustrating the changes over the last month since she'd started working with the baby. Finally she ended the presentation—which ended her consulting job for this group, as well. "My recommendation is that you not place George in a regular foster care situation for a while yet. We think of bonding as a natural human need, but George's situation is more complex than that. If you want this little angel to make it, we need him connected 24/7 to a warm, human body—and I mean that literally. We have to force him to trust, because even at this young age, he has learned to survive by tuning out. He simply won't take the chance of trusting anyone—unless we put him in a situation where he's forced to."

Halfway through the meeting, the social worker tiptoed in late. Phoebe saw skepticism in the neurologist's face, dubiousness in the social worker's. She didn't mind. The docs wanted to be able to prescribe medicine that would promptly fix the baby. The social worker wanted to foster the baby out and get him off her hands.

Everybody wanted easy answers. Phoebe could only seem to come up with time-consuming, expensive and inconvenient answers, which not only regularly annoyed everyone, but also tended to go down harder because they came from an upstart, redheaded, five-foot, three-inch baby masseuse.

No one ever heard of a baby masseuse when she came to Gold River. No one ever heard of it in Asheville, either, where she'd started out. Heaven knew, she'd never wanted to create a job that didn't exist. But darn it, she'd kept running across throwaway babies that the system had only lazy, lousy, inadequate answers for. It wasn't her fault that her unorthodox ideas worked. It wasn't her fault she fought like a shrew for the little ones, either.

When it came down to it, maybe she'd just found her calling. Yelling and arguing seemed to come to her naturally.

When the meeting broke up around four, the powers that be tore out as if released from prison. Phoebe started hum-

ming under her breath—she'd won the program for Baby
George—further proof that it paid to be a shrew. And now,
because the meeting ended early, she could get home and give
the dogs a run before dinner.

She pushed on her shoes, grabbed her black-sashed jacket,
but she couldn't take off until she put on some lip gloss. Talking always made her lips dry. She found at least a half-dozen
glosses and lipsticks in the dark depths of her bag, but she
wanted the raspberry gloss that went with her sweater. And
then…

"Ms. Schneider? Phoebe Schneider?"

She spun around, the tube of raspberry gloss still open in
her hand. Two men stood in the double doorway—in fact, the
two of them blocked the entrance with the effectiveness of a
Mack truck. Positively they weren't hospital staff. For sure
Gold River Memorial Hospital had some adorable doctors,
but she knew none with barn-beam shoulders and lumberjack
muscles.

"Yeah, I'm Phoebe."

When they immediately charged toward her, she had to
control the impulse to bolt. Obviously they couldn't help
being giants, any more than she could help being undersize.
It wasn't their fault they were sexy lugs, either, from their
sandy hair to their sharp, clean-cut looks to their broody dark
eyes…any more than she could help having the personality
of a bulldog. Or so some said. Personally, Phoebe thought she
was pretty darn nice. Under certain circumstances. When she
had time. "I take it you're looking for me."

The tallest one—the one in the serious gray suit—answered first. "Yeah. We want to hire you for our brother."

"Your brother," she echoed. She got the lip gloss capped,

just in time to drop it. The one in the sweatshirt and jeans hunkered down to retrieve it for her.

"Yes. I'm Ben Lockwood, and this is my brother Harry."

"Lockwood? As in Lockwood Restaurant?" The town of Gold River had lots of restaurants, but none as posh as Lockwood's. For that matter, the Lockwood name had an automatic association to old money and old gold, which was probably why Phoebe had never run into them before.

Ben, the one in the suit, answered first. "Yeah. That's Harry's place. He's the chef in the family. I'm the builder. And our youngest brother is Fergus. He's the one we want to hire you for."

Phoebe felt a familiar wearisome thud in her stomach. Guys. Looking to hire a masseuse. For another guy. One plus one invariably added up to someone thinking she hired out for services above and beyond massaging.

Still, she didn't waste time getting defensive, just gathered her gear and headed out. The men trailed after her down the hall toward the east entrance. Harry grabbed her box of slides—which tried to tip when she pushed open the door. "I don't know why you two didn't just call. I'm listed. And then I could have told you right off that I only work with babies."

Ben had a ready answer. "We didn't call because we were afraid you'd brush us off. And we know you work with little kids and babies now, but the hospital said you were a licensed physical therapist, the best they'd ever seen. Fox is in a special situation. So we hoped you might consider making an exception for him."

There was no way she was taking on an adult male. None. Phoebe wasn't short on courage, but her heart had been smashed too hard from a close encounter with the wrong kind. She would take another chance. Sometime in the next decade. But for now, the only risks she willingly took were for babies.

None of that was any of their business, of course. She just told them she was booked up the wazoo for months—which had the effect of swatting a fly. Ignoring her protest completely, they trailed her through the parking lot like puppies—giant, overgrown puppies—carrying her bags and boxes, picking up the stuff she dropped, flanking her like bodyguards.

Typical of February in North Carolina—at least in the mountains—evening was falling faster than a stone. The afternoon's brisk wind had turned noisy and blustery, and the clouds were puffing in hard now. In another month or so, magnolias and rhododendron would furiously flower on the elegant hospital grounds, but right now, even the sentinel oaks weren't gutsy enough to leaf out yet. The wind shivered through her long auburn braid, teasing at the ribbon wrapped through it and threatening to unravel it.

The guys were starting to unravel her, too—but not for the reasons she'd first feared. By the time they reached her old white van in the third row, she had the ghastly feeling that she'd fallen totally in love with both of them. They looked at her as if she were a goddess. That helped. They treated her as if she were a hero. She liked that, too. Mostly, though, she had a strong sixth sense about predators. These two were just plain good guys. How was she supposed to resist that?

"Ben, Harry…look. I don't know if the hospital misled you, but I don't do any regular physical therapy anymore. I just don't have time. And besides that, if your brother has some kind of special problems, I have no qualifications to help him."

"Yeah, well, Fox has been to tons of people with blue-ribbon qualifications. Doctors. Psychiatrists. Specialized physical therapists. Hell, we even brought in a priest and we're not Catholic." Ben made the joke but then couldn't pull off a smile. "We have to try something different. We're losing our brother. We need some fresh ideas, a different outlook. If you'd just take a look at him—"

Sometime over the next ten minutes. Phoebe picked up that the Lockwood brothers regularly referred to themselves as animals. Ben was Bear. Harry was Moose. And they called their youngest brother Fox.

She loved animals. Wild or tame. And the Lockwood brothers had clearly dropped their jobs and lives to come here and gang up on her, which said something about how much they loved their brother. "Honest to Pete, I'm telling you straight, I can't help you. I would if I could."

"Just come and meet him."

"I can't."

"We haven't explained what he's been through yet. At least listen. And then if you can't help, you can't. We're just asking you to *try*."

"Guys. *I can't*."

"Just one shot. A few minutes. We'll pay you five hundred bucks for a half hour, how's that? I swear, if you decide you can't help him after that, we'll never bug you again. You have our word."

My God. They wheedled and whined and charmed and bribed. Phoebe rarely met anyone who could outstubborn her, but these two were beyond blockheaded. Still. If she took on one adult patient, it would open the door to being asked again. And that wasn't worth the risk.

"I'm sorry, guys, but no," she said firmly.

At seven o'clock that night, Phoebe flipped the gearshift in reverse and barreled out of her driveway. "I don't want to hear any grief," she told the dogs sharing the passenger seat. "A woman has a right to change her mind."

Neither Mop nor Duster argued. As long as they got to ride in the van with their noses out the window, they never cared what she said.

"You two just stick by me. If something feels hinky, then we'll all take off together. Got it?"

Again, neither mutt responded. Even after two years, Phoebe wasn't dead positive who'd rescued whom. The two pint-size dirty-white mop heads had shown up at her back door when she first moved to Gold River. They'd been scrawny and matted and starved. Throwaways. Yet ever since they'd acted as if she was the throwaway and they were the benevolent adopters. It boggled the mind.

"The brothers really were okay. I know, I know, they were men. And who can trust anyone stuck with all that testosterone? But really, the situation isn't what I first thought. Their brother sounds as if he's in rough shape. So even if I can't do anything, it just seemed heartless to keep saying no."

Again the mutts offered no input. They were both hanging out the open window, their bitsy tongues lolling, paying her no attention whosoever.

Before the sun completely dropped, lights popped on all down Main Street. Wrought-iron carriage lamps lined the shopping district. If she hadn't agreed to this darn fool meeting, she could have been suckered into the shoe sale at Well

Heeled, or accidentally slipped into TJ Maxx. Well, it was hard to slip into TJ accidentally when the store was two blocks away, but the principle was still valid.

Worry started circling her mood. She loved her work. The bank claimed she was a long way from solvent, but money wasn't that important to her. Doing something that mattered was. She'd found a touch therapy for babies with unique problems that really worked. Babies were her niche.

Men weren't.

She liked guys. Always had, always would. But she'd met Alan even *before* she'd hung up the masseuse sign, when she'd still been a physical therapist. He'd been a patient recovering from a serious bone break. Right off he'd judged her as a hedonist and a sensualist—a woman who loved to touch. And he'd loved those qualities in her.

He'd said.

He'd also claimed she was the hottest woman he'd ever met. He'd even said that as if it were a compliment. In the beginning.

Edgily she gnawed on a thumbnail. She'd moved to Gold River to obliterate those painful memories and start over. She'd done just that. Her whole life was on an uphill track again—but she also had good reason to be careful.

Those darn Lockwood brothers had sabotaged her common sense by painting a picture in her mind. A picture of their brother. A picture she just couldn't seem to shake.

Apparently this Fergus had volunteered to serve in the military and came home with a medical discharge because of injuries sustained from a "dirty bomb." The Veterans' Hospital had patched him up and eventually released him. Both Ben and Harry agreed that their brother had initially seemed fine, weak but definitely recovering. Only, he'd increasingly withdrawn after coming home. The family tried bringing additional doctors and psychologists into the picture, but Fergus had basically shut the door and shut down. No one could get through to him.

The brothers claimed they'd heard about her through a doctor friend—a woman who'd said she had the touch of a healer with babies. That was an exaggeration, of course. Phoebe couldn't heal anyone. Certainly not anyone as damaged and traumatized as this Fergus sounded.

She'd lowered her defenses when it became obvious the guys weren't looking for sex, surrogate sex, or any of the other ridiculous things guys assumed masseuses really were. But now she felt unsure again. Their brother had been through something terrible. He likely had post-traumatic stress syndrome or whatever that was called. It was sad and it was awful—but she had no knowledge or skills to help someone in that kind of situation.

When it came down to it, she'd only agreed to come because she was a complete dolt. The brothers had been so darling that she just couldn't find a way to say no.

She suddenly realized that the slip of paper with the address was no longer on the seat, but had been stolen. "Damn it, Mop! Give it!"

Mop coughed up the damp, chewed piece of paper. Thankfully the number on the address was still legible. At the next right, she turned on Magnolia, left three blocks later on Willow, then followed the hillside climb. In theory she knew where the rich lived. She just never had an excuse to dawdle in their neighborhood.

A handful of mansions perched on the cliff, overlooking

the river below where their grandfathers had once scooped up fortunes in gold. The homes were hidden behind high fences and wrought-iron gates. Still, the hardwoods were stripped bare at this time of year, so Phoebe could catch fleeting glimpses of the gorgeous homes. Most were built of the local stone and marble, with big, wraparound verandas and lush landscaping.

The Lockwood house was tucked in the curve of a secluded cul de sac. Feeling like a trespasser, she drove past the gates, past the two-story house and five-car garage—as instructed—and pulled up to a smaller home beyond. The brothers had called it the bachelor house, which was apparently a historical term—a place where the young unmarried men hung out before they were married, where they could sow wild oats away from their mother's judgmental eyes. The concept sounded distinctly decadent and Southern to Phoebe, but the point was that Fergus had been living there since he got out of the hospital, according to his brothers.

Close up, the main house didn't look so ritzy as it did sturdy and lived in, with cheerful lights beaming from all the windows downstairs. By contrast, only a single light shone from the bachelor house, making the place look dark and gloomy and ghostly.

She *liked* ghost stories, she reminded herself, besides which it was too late to chicken out now. Before she could open the door and climb out, the back porch light popped on, so the brothers must have been watching for her. Mop and Duster bounded off her lap and galloped for the shadows, promptly peed and then zoomed straight for the guys in the doorway. Phoebe followed more slowly. The same Lockwood brothers who'd charmed the devil out of her were already giving the girls a thorough petting, but they stood up and turned serious the instant she approached.

"I'll pay you up-front," Harry said quietly.

"Oh, shut up," she said crossly. "I told you that five hundred dollars was ridiculous. I don't do bribes." She added firmly, "I don't do miracles, either."

"That's not what we heard."

"Well, you heard wrong. This is so out of my league. Your brother's going to think you're nuts for bringing in a masseuse. And I do, too."

Neither brother argued with her—they'd already been over all that ground—Ben just motioned her in. The dogs frisked ahead.

It wasn't her kind of decor, yet right off the place drew her. The kitchen was cluttered with plates and containers of food—none of which looked touched—but beyond the debris were lead-paned glass cupboards and a slate sink and a clay-tiled floor. She had to identify things by gleams of reflected light, since apparently no one believed in turning on lights around here.

Beyond the kitchen were doors leading to a utility room and bathroom and eventually a bedroom or two, she guessed. But off to the right was the living room. She caught a glimpse of stuccoed walls and an arched fieldstone fireplace before she heard a gruff, *"What the hell?"*

So. Not hard to guess that the dogs were already introducing themselves to Fergus.

She trailed after them, finally locating the one light source—a single reading lamp outfitted with a nominal fifteen-watt bulb. Still, even in the gloom, she easily identified the living room as a testosterone den. No frou-frou had ever crossed this threshold. From the dark wood to the shutters to the hardwood floors, it was a guy's place all the way. The couch and chairs were upholstered in a deep claret red, the coffee table chosen to tolerate boots and glass marks. The room smelled of dust and last night's whiskey and silence.

She heard the brothers talking in the kitchen, guessed they wouldn't lag behind more than a few moments. In those spare seconds, though, the lonely stillness of the room tugged at her…and yeah, so did the body on the couch.

At first look, if her hormones had perked to attention, she just might have turned tail and run. That was the threat, of course. That she'd care about a man who would hurt her again—who'd form preconceptions about her and her profession, who'd judge her based on surface impressions. But that wasn't going to happen. Not with this man.

Fergus was clearly so safe that her defenses dropped faster than a drawbridge for a castle. He wasn't going to hurt her. Or care about her. Those were absolute "for sures."

Aw, man.

Just one look made her heart fill up with blade-deep compassion.

She'd assumed he'd be good-looking because Bear and Moose were such studs. Instead, he was longer than Lincoln and scrawny. Dark eyes were deeply set in a sharp boned face with a slash of a mouth and a square jaw. He had his brothers' barn-beam shoulders, but his jeans and shirt hung on him. His brothers both had charm in their smiles, creases in their cheeks from laugh lines. Fergus, damn him, had so much pain in his eyes that Phoebe had to suck in a breath.

She only had that brief moment to study him—and to realize that her two fluff balls were curled on his chest—before he spotted her in the doorway.

He didn't acknowledge her. He just said, "Bear. Moose. Get her out of here."

He didn't yell it. His voice wasn't remotely rude. It was just dead cold and exhausted. Both brothers emerged from the kitchen fast and barreled in. "Take it easy, Fox. We were just getting some drinks from the kitchen. We just wanted to have a talk—"

Maybe Fergus was the youngest of the three—and for damn sure, the weakest—yet somehow he came across as the family CEO. "Forget it. I don't know what you two thought you were setting up, but it's not going to happen. All of you, just get out of here. Leave me alone."

Phoebe found it fascinating, watching the two big, brawny guys try to bully their prostrate brother. That flower just wasn't gonna bloom. Who'd have guessed the skinny, surly, mean-eyed Fox could express authority, much less win, against the powerful good guys?

But that wasn't the reason her heart was suddenly pounding like a manic drum.

Phoebe took another quiet step closer. The longer she studied him, the more she realized that he'd never actually looked at her. Or his brothers. She doubted he was seeing much of anything. His eyes were smudged with weariness, and his skin wasn't just gray because of the dim light. He was shocky from pain. Even trying to speak in that dead-quiet whisper seemed to sharpen the fierce, dark light in his eyes.

Worse than that, she saw one of his hands on Mop. They knew. Both her mutts always knew which humans to avoid and which humans needed attention from them. They were

hell on wheels and nonstop nuisances, but they somehow responded instinctively to people in pain.

Now she understood why the place was so dungeon dark.
Light undoubtedly made the hurt worse.

Phoebe told herself that her pulse was rushing hard for the
obvious reason. She cared. She could no more stop herself
from responding to someone suffering than she could stop
breathing. It wasn't a response to him as a *man*. She didn't
have to worry about that, she was positive. But just as positively, she could no more walk out on a human in pain than
she could quit breathing.

She started by pushing between the two brothers. "You
two, head outside for a few minutes, okay? Let me talk to Fergus alone. Mop. Duster. Lay down, girls."

The dogs immediately obeyed her, but the boys weren't
quite so easy to order around. Harry—Moose—looked un-
certainly at Bear. "Maybe we were wrong," he said unhap-
pily. "I don't think it's a good idea for us to completely leave
you alone with—"

"It's all right," she assured him, as she herded them both
toward the door.

Of course, it wasn't quite that easy. The brothers warily
agreed to leave her alone for a short stretch with Fergus, but
the instant the back door closed, the house was suddenly silent as sin. A goofy little shiver chased up her spine—until
she returned to the living room.

From the doorway she caught the gleam of Fergus's
broody, angry eyes and almost immediately relaxed.

Phoebe was only a coward about one thing.

This wasn't it.

Nice guys she had to worry about. But a tortured, mean-tempered crabby pistol like Fergus, she could handle in her sleep. The poor guy just didn't realize who his brothers had brought home to dinner.

Two

"**F**ergus…my name is Phoebe Schneider. Your brothers asked me to come here."

He heard the voice and he saw her as a shadow, but it was like trying to process information through a fog. Trying to focus hurt. Trying to talk hurt. Hell, trying to breathe seemed to set off new knives in his temples. "I don't care who you are. Just go *away*."

There seemed to be a dog—or two—on his chest. A wet nose had snuffled under his palm. It was odd, but he didn't mind. Maybe it was the surprise of feeling the pups' warmth, their thick scruffy fur under his fingers. But then the woman quietly ordered them to the ground, and they immediately obeyed her.

"Honestly, I'd love to take off, Fergus. I never wanted to come here to begin with. This is crazy, right? Why would you want a stranger around when you don't feel well? But your brothers are rock-headed bullies. They got it in their minds that I can help you, and they're just going to badger both of us unless I at least *try*."

The headaches always seemed to come with memory flashes. The little boy with the dark hair and beautiful, big, sad eyes. Shyly coming up to him. Taking the candy bar. Then…the explosion.

Over and over the headaches repeated the same pattern, the explosion in his memory echoing the explosions of pain. Sometimes, like now, he literally saw stars. Ironically they were downright beautiful, a dazzling aura of lightning-silver lights that would have been mesmerizing if a sledgehammer hadn't been pounding in his temples. And, yeah, he heard the woman talking. Her voice was velvet low, sexy soft, soothing. Most of her words didn't register, because nothing was registering in his brain right then. But she was still there. *That* got through.

He heard a small plop of sound, like a jacket or sweater being dropped. And there were suddenly new, vague scents in the room—camellias, strawberries, oranges. And through the scissor-slashing pain, he thought he caught a glimpse of long, dark-cinnamon-red hair.

When the headaches got this bad, though, he was never sure what was reality and what was hallucination.

"I don't want you to waste energy talking," she continued quietly. "But I need to know what these headaches are about. Your brothers told me you were recovering from injuries. So, did you get hit on your head or your neck? Is that the cause of the pain?"

He tried to answer without moving his lips. "No. I've got

dirty bomb parts sticking out all over my body. But not my neck. Not my head. Hell." He squeezed his eyes closed, clenched his teeth. "No more talking. Go away."

"I will," she promised him blithely, but then didn't. "So this is a migraine?"

He didn't answer, but that didn't seem to deter her.

"If it's a migraine, you've surely had a doctor prescribe some serious pain medication for you...."

It was like ignoring taxes. It didn't work. So he tried answering her again. "I have buckets full of pills. Ergotamine. Beta-blockers. Calcium channel blocker. Codeine—" Hell. Even talking this quietly jostled new razor-edged nerve endings. "Quit taking them all. Don't help. Only make me throw up. Then it's worse..."

Alarmed, he realized she was coming closer. She definitely had long, cinnamon-red hair. Other impressions bombarded him—that strawberry scent and hint of camellias. A wide, sensual mouth. Snapping clear eyes. Blue eyes. Too blue.

"Get out," he said. If he had to throw her out, he would. He'd undoubtedly hurl if he tried any real physical movement, end up shaking and sick from the exertion, but this time he meant it. He'd had enough.

Finally she seemed to get it, because she obeyed and turned around. He heard the soft footfalls, heard the distant sound of the back door opening, his brothers' voices, then the door closing again.

The sudden silence should have given him peace, but it wasn't that easy. He concentrated on closing his eyes, not moving, not thinking, not breathing any more than he had to. But the little boy's face kept showing up in his mind. A child.

A young child. Like all the young children he used to teach. And the drum thudding in his brain sounded like a judge's gavel, as if he were being accused of a nameless crime, as if he'd been found guilty without ever having a chance to defend himself.

He was sinking deeper into the pain when he heard her voice again—her voice, her sounds, her presence and, yeah, her dogs. One leaped on his stomach, tried to nuzzle under his hand.

"Down, Mop," she whispered, and again the scruffy pup immediately obeyed. As if she thought he could conceivably be interested, she started chitchatting in that velvet-low voice. "Normally I work at home, so the dogs are used to being with me. And I do leave them sometimes. They've got a dog door and a big, fenced-in backyard. But the thing is, they just hate it when I leave in the evening, so I tend to bring them if I possibly can."

"No." This had gone on far enough. He got it now—the purpose of the casual chitchat had been to distract him from whatever the Sam Hill she was doing. He heard rustling sounds behind him, smelled more odd, evocative fragrances, then heard the strike of a match. When she turned off the lamp, the only light in the room came from the teardrop flames of a few candles. The darkness was much easier on his eyes, his head, only the rest of the smells and sounds made no sense. They weren't bad sensations. They were just alien to the house and him.

"Close your eyes," she repeated.

"No. Why? For God's sake, do I have to get up and throw you out of the house to get you to leave?"

"Fox," she said gently, "close your damn eyes and quit

fighting me. I'm nobody you need to worry about. Just shut up and let go."

That was such a ridiculous thing for a stranger to say that momentarily he was too startled to respond. Even the memory flashes disappeared. He tried to concentrate, because he was determined to push past the pain and get up. She was leaving. He figured she had to be some kind of medical do-gooder his brothers had brought in, but it didn't make any difference. He was a pinch away from losing his cookies. His only hope was staying so still that the pain got no worse.

Except that he had to get rid of the redhead first. "You're all done, lady. I don't know what the hell you...I...oh. Oh. Oh, God."

She touched him.

She was behind him, out of sight, must have knelt down right at his head, because he felt her hands on his temples. Cool, smooth fingers whispered on his temples and forehead. There was a substance on her hands—something slippery that smelled like Creamsicles. She stroked the narrow spot below his eyebrows, then the vee above his nose, then soothed that light-scented oil into his forehead, into his hairline.

He opened his mouth to swear at her again, even got out the 'f' sound of the word he furiously wanted to express...only he forgot.

He meant to swear, he really did, but nothing came out but a groan.

A weak, vulnerable groan. Exasperated, he tried to do the cussing thing again, only to repeat the same problem. He forgot.

Her fingers sifted into his short, coarse hair, fingertips

gently massaging the skin, the pads of the fingers soothing, smoothing. The slick, soft stuff went into his hair, into his scalp. He didn't care.

"I can't make a migraine go away," she said quietly. "But if we can get you to relax, you'll have a shot at sleeping it off. You're so tense with the pain, it's making it worse. But it's hard to work on you while you're lying on this couch. Especially with all your clothes on. If you could just shift forward a little, the couch arm wouldn't be in our way so much…"

He stopped listening to her. He couldn't listen. He was too busy feeling.

She couldn't physically move him—hell, he had to be twice her size. But somehow she made the couch pillow disappear, so that she could lean over and contact him more directly. She worked, and kept working, behind his ears, down the sides of his neck.

She stopped to get more of that smelly Creamsicle stuff, came back, shivered it through his hair, scraped it through his scalp, rubbed it, kneaded it, soothed it, caressed it.

The more she worked, the more he felt a deep, sexual pull in the pit of his belly. Nothing she was doing was sexual. She never touched him below the neck and, hell, she was getting that gooey slippery stuff all over his head.

But it seemed as if she pulled the pain right out of him.

His headache didn't instantly disappear. But the sensations she invoked seemed bigger than the pain, big enough to distract him, big enough to suck him under a sleek, silent, shimmering wave of sensation.

She started humming under her breath, an old song. "Summertime." About how living was easy and the cotton was high. She couldn't hum. Her voice was so off-key it should have grated on his nerves—and God knew, his nerves had been in shreds for hours.

But not anymore. The soft pads of her thumbs stroked his closed eyes, so lightly it was like being stroked by a skein of silk. She brushed his cheekbones, remolded them, scrolled down to his jawline, pushed, stroked, pulled.

He suddenly went hard—which was as impossible as a phoenix rising. No man could get a hard-on with a migraine. The thought was ludicrous.

But damn...he'd never had a woman touch him this way. He'd never had a woman *own* him this way. He'd never felt this...connection. As if someone else really were on the other side of the dark abyss and he wasn't alone, not anymore, as if she knew intimate things about his feelings that no one else ever had.

It was petrifying.

He didn't let other people in. Or he hadn't, since coming back from the Middle East. His life had irrevocably changed. He just wanted to be left the total hell alone—and he didn't want her near him, either, but hell.

He felt himself slipping and then slipping further. Into her spell. Under her spell.

She could have done anything, said anything she wanted—as long as she kept touching him. All the P.T. and rehab and rebuilding he'd been through over these last months—yeah, he'd survived it all, willing or not, but nothing had dented the pain. Nothing had come close.

Until her.

His eyes were already closed, but he could feel sleep coming. Real sleep. Not the kind where he'd wake up in an hour, soaked in sweat, heart pounding, screams and explosions and the indelible face of a little boy relentlessly in his head. But the other kind of sleep. The kind where you sank into a deep, safe stillness and felt free enough to…just…let…go.

Mop and Duster lifted their heads when Phoebe snuffed out the candles. She waited a moment for her eyes to adjust to the darkness and then quietly picked up her jacket and gear. She tiptoed through the silent house, trying to make no sound until she stepped foot outside.

Ben and Harry were still there, waiting for her, pacing back and forth the length of the veranda.

"I'll be damned. He didn't kill you."

She thought that was a particularly perceptive comment of Ben's. "He's sound asleep."

Both brothers shook their heads. "He can't be. He doesn't sleep anymore. In fact, that's part of the problem— he's so damn surly because he can't get any rest—"

"Well, he's out for the count now. And hopefully he'll stay asleep until he can clock up some serious rest." Phoebe took a moment to inhale a deep, long breath. She had no idea how long she'd been inside, but the sky was now blacker than pitch and the bushes covered with a fresh coat of rime. She let the dogs chase off into the darkness to do their business. It gave her another moment.

Right then she seemed to need about fifty moments. Typically her hands could tremble for a while after the intense, hard work of a serious massage. Tonight, though, she knew there was another reason for her shakiness—a reason that badly unsettled her. Complicating her concern, the Lockwood brothers were looking at her as if she were a goddess.

"It wasn't anything special I did," she told them promptly. "I can't cure anyone's migraine. It's just that the best 'fix' for people who have headaches like that is to get them to sleep, any way and any how you can. At least, that I've found. Anybody could have done what I did."

"But no one else has. And you can't imagine all the people who've seen—"

She wasn't going to argue with the two big lugs, not after an impossibly long day. Right now, besides, her knees were moaning and groaning from kneeling so long for Fox. And her hands…her hands still felt him. "Look, I'm pretty sure he'll be better when he wakes up—as long as he gets a few hours of solid sleep—but does he live here alone?"

"Yeah." Harry motioned to the big house. "Our mom has been living there alone since Dad died. We all moved out after we grew up. Normally Ben has a place in the country and I live over my restaurant. The bachelor house was empty for years. But Fox gave up his apartment when he went into the military—didn't make sense to pay rent when he figured he was going to be gone for several years. The point, though, is that when he came home all beat up, the bachelor house seemed an ideal place for him to hole up, close to family."

Ben filled in more. "We've been hanging close for the last two months. Fergus won't let anyone stay with him, but the idiot is in no position to take care of himself, and for darn sure, mom can't cope with him alone."

"Hell, we can't cope with him, either," Harry said. "I can't believe you got him to sleep—"

"Don't." They kept looking at her as if she were an angel, which was funny and fun but too ridiculous to tolerate any longer. "I just got here at the right time, that's all. He was probably on the other side of the headache, ready to sleep."

"The hell he was," Ben said peaceably.

"Yeah, well, I won't be coming back, so don't even try going there. He made it more than clear that he didn't want me around, so this was definitely a one-shot deal."

"But you'd come back if he asked?"

"He won't ask." She opened the van door. The pups leaped in.

"But if he did ask—"

"Yeah, then…*maybe.* If I could make it fit with my schedule. If I thought he was asking, and not you two pushing the idea on him. If…" She dug in her purse for her keys. Not that she carried a big bag, but she could probably have survived for six months in Europe on what she considered emergency supplies. Eventually her fingers emerged with the keys—and when she looked up, suddenly the two giants were descending on her, grinning ear to ear. She got a smooch on both cheeks before she could stop them.

"*Thanks,* Phoebe. We love you."

Color bloomed in her cheeks. "You guys," she began, and then just shook her head and climbed into the van.

Until she turned out of the driveway and disappeared into the dark night, her shoulders were knotted up with tension. Slowly, though, she felt her muscles—and heart—start to simmer down.

Touch was erotic. That's just the way it was. She couldn't touch someone—intensely touch, the kind of touch required if you really wanted to help the person—without responding herself.

So. Helping Fergus had turned her on. Nothing new about that. Nothing interesting.

Nothing she needed to be afraid of.

"Right, girls?" she asked the pups.

The dogs looked up, as if trying to reassure her, yet she still seemed to need to take in heaping gulps of fresh air.

It was Alan who'd made her feel cheap and immoral. Sleazy. As if sexuality and sensuality were a weakness in her character that made her less than decent. She knew that was crap. She *knew,* but, damn, the residue of hurt was harder to shake than a flu germ, even after all this time.

In her head and her heart, she'd believed forever that touch was the most powerful sense. Almost everyone responded to being touched—the right kind of touch. People could go hungry, could go without sleep, could suffer all kinds of deprivation.

But people who went without touch for a long period seemed to lose part of themselves.

Phoebe understood perfectly well that touch in itself couldn't heal anything. Touch just seemed to enable a body to *want* to heal itself. It seemed to help a body rest. It seemed to remind even the lost souls that there was wonder on the other side of loneliness—the wonder of connecting, of finding someone else who reached you emotionally.

She pulled in her driveway, past the softly lit sign:

BABY LOVE
Phoebe Schneider, Licensed PT, Licensed LMBT, ABW, MP
Infant Massage Therapy

She docked the van in the narrow driveway, turned the key and leaned back. The sign was the key, she realized.

She just had to quit thinking of Fergus Lockwood as a man—and think of him as if he were another one of her baby clients.

Actually, he struck her very much like one of her lost babies—as if he'd been deprived of touch. As if he'd lost touch with himself because he'd become so isolated from human contact. In fact, as if he needed touch so badly that he'd responded fiercely and evocatively to any contact.

In other words, he'd never been responding to her as a woman.

She climbed out of the van, only to suffer a traffic jam at the back door with the pooches trying to barrel in ahead of her. It was after bedtime, after all. "So that's the deal, girls," she told them. "He's not likely to call again, but in case he does, that's how we handle it. We just think of him as one of our babies."

She flipped on the light and plunked down her purse. A vision immediately filled her mind of rolling smooth muscles, sleek warm skin, fierce dark eyes. She swallowed, and thought babies—yeah, right.

By Sunday afternoon, when she pulled into the parking lot for Young at Heart, Gold River's home for the elderly, she'd totally and completely forgotten about Fergus.

A domineering, macho wind was hurling down from the mountain, throwing handfuls of confetti snow here and there and burning her lungs. It was the kind of afternoon when she just wanted to snuggle in a down comforter with two dogs, a book, a chick flick and a mug of hot chocolate—with melted marshmallows.

She wondered—just idly, since she'd completely stopped

thinking about him—whether Fergus might be tempted by a small, sizzling fire on a cuddly cold afternoon.

There was a lot more wrong with him than the debilitating headaches, Bear and Moose had told her. He'd been home from the hospital for two months, yet except for short grocery runs, stayed locked in. Didn't see people. Didn't return calls. Didn't *do* anything.

She had no idea what he'd done before—for a living or for hobbies or anything else—but obviously they were describing a problem with depression. Maybe the depression was a result of his experience in the military. Maybe it was from injuries that refused to heal—chronic pain could cripple the strongest optimist. The thing was, it was hard to help someone without knowing specifically what was wrong with them. You had to have some clue what motivated the individual.

Not that she was thinking about what might motivate Fergus.

She wasn't thinking about him at all.

"Hey, Phoebe!"

"Hey, handsome." Typically she was effusively greeted the instant she walked into the rest home—as were the dogs, who were as welcomed here on Sunday afternoons as she was. In principle she had her hands full with her baby clients, but the manager of the rest home had somehow conned her into regular weekend visits. She hadn't said yes because she was a sucker or weak-willed or anything like that. She just hadn't quite known how to say no.

Barney—who she invariably called Handsome—was ninety-three and skinnier than a stick, but he still had a full head of fluffy white hair. He could walk with a cane, although he couldn't stop his hands from shaking anymore. The dogs piled over to greet him, as did Phoebe, who enthusiastically—if carefully—pecked him on the cheek.

"I swear," she whispered, "you're so good-looking, I think we should run away from this place and have a wild, crazy affair."

"Go on with you. You're young and beautiful—"

"And you're not?" She raised her eyebrows and patted him on the fanny—which he loved—and then she moved on.

The bad wing was on the west side. She always started there. No one seemed to touch the end-stage patients but the nurses. The staff offered necessary care and caring, but no one had time to express affection or gentleness.

Mop and Duster were allowed on the beds—encouraged, in fact. Even the Alzheimer's group roused to pet a dog. She brushed hair, rubbed shoulders and necks, massaged cheeks, patted, soaked feet and hands. Some didn't respond. But some always did.

An hour later she hit the east wing—which was definitely more of a kick-ass crowd. They fought over the dogs, chattered nonstop, bent her ear with their endless array of health complaints.

She couldn't help loving them. They made her feel so needed.

Most had lost the spouse who would have still touched them, and other living family seemed afraid of their brittle bones. They were so hungry to hold hands, to feel a cheek against theirs, to stroke and hold and hug.

The manager at Young at Heart had repeatedly begged Phoebe to go on retainer for them as a regular. He claimed the whole place perked up after one of her visits; she made that much difference in health and morale.

That was nonsense, of course. But for the next couple hours, she was busier than a one-armed bandit. She washed Willa's hair—not because the rest home didn't have a regular hairdresser, but because Willa adored the head massage. Who didn't, Phoebe thought....

Which reminded her again of how Fergus had responded to even the most basic massage techniques. The Lockwood brothers had confused her by intimating Fergus was unreachable. Cripes, he'd melted faster than a sundae in the sun.

It kept coming back to her...the feeling of his scalp in her hands, the short hair shivering through her fingers...but the best had been that one moment when she finally felt the tension in his muscles let go, let go, slow as a shadow, the pain in those beautiful eyes finally easing.

"How come some nice man hasn't snapped you up?" Martha always asked, invariably, like now, when Phoebe was soaking her feet in a baby oil and clove mixture. "I just can't understanding it. You're so pretty, with all that gorgeous red hair—"

"I came close to marriage one time." She gave the standard answer, standard smile, standard laugh. "But thankfully I escaped that fate worse than death by moving here."

"You won't be singing that tune forever," Martha said shrewdly. "He just wasn't the right one. But it just makes no sense. The men should be pounding on your door."

"Nah. I think word's spread that I'm a mouthy, bossy troublemaker."

Gus, who only asked one thing from her every week—to sit in the TV room holding hands for ten minutes with a dog on his lap—piped in, "I'll marry you, Phoebe. You can have all my money."

"I'd marry you for love anyday, you sweetie pie. I don't want your money."

"A looker like you should be more greedy. Nobody can survive in this world without a little selfishness in their soul. You gotta think about taking care of yourself. Looking out for number one."

It was funny, she thought, how easy it was to fool people. She'd never have done this kind of work if it didn't give back to her tenfold. The truth was, she was selfish and greedy and she always put herself first. And she proved it when her cell phone sang on her way home.

It was Harry Lockwood. "Could you come for Fergus again?"

"Can't." Her answer came out sure as sunshine.

"He asked for you."

She believed that like she'd believed at fifteen when her date swore he'd stop, promise, hope to die. "Look, if Fergus calls and asks me to come, I'll set up a time with him. But it's Sunday night. I haven't had any dinner. I have to wash my hair, get my stuff together for the week, groom the dogs. Sunday nights are sacred, you know?"

"This is about hair?"

"No. It's about my not believing your brother asked for me."

"Okay," Harry said, and hung up.

The cell phone rang again just as she was pulling into her driveway. "Phoebe? Did I mention the last time I saw you that I'm deeply and hopelessly in love with you?"

She laughed even before she recognized Ben's voice. "I swear, the two of you are bad to the bone. But the answer is no. Absolutely no. I'm not intruding on Fergus again unless he specifically wants my help."

Ben went on as if she'd never spoken. "I've never been tempted to marry, but then I saw you. I've always been a fanny man, and your darling little butt is really the best I've ever—"

She shook her head. "Hey! That's fighting really dirty."

"We have to fight dirty, Phoebe. Fox is in real trouble. He was doing fine for a couple days after you left, most of the week, in fact. But now I don't think he's slept a wink in the past forty-eight hours. If you'd just known him before this all happened—Fergus was always full of the devil, never sat still a minute in his life. He was interested in everything, active in sports and hobbies and the community. And kids. God, he loves kids. You can't even imagine how good he is with kids. So to see him sitting in that dark room, doing nothing, not wanting to do anything—"

"Come *on*, Ben. If you brothers are close and he won't listen to you, why on earth would you think I could do anything? I can't just go over there and bully him—"

"You did before."

"He had such a bad headache before that he'd have let in the devil if it could have helped him."

"We tried the devil. We've tried everything. You're the only one who even dented that pain of his." Ben cleared his throat. "Harry said you had to wash your hair."

She knew that tone. It was one of those male "I'll be understanding about this ridiculous female thinking" tone.

"Harry also mentioned that possibly you might want a year's worth of free dinners. And I was thinking—I don't know where you live—but I told you I was the builder in the clan. I never met a woman who didn't want her kitchen redone—"

"Oh, for God's sake. This is ridiculous."

"And while I was fixing your kitchen, you could eat at Harry's restaurant—"

"Stop! I don't want to hear another word!"

"Does that mean you're coming?"

Three

Fox closed his eyes and stood absolutely still under the pelting-hot shower spray.

Maybe he'd given up sleeping and eating and couldn't get his life back for love or money. But nothing kept him from showering once a day and sometimes twice.

Even after all these weeks, parts kept coming out of him. The doctors claimed that's how it was with dirty bombs. Something new needled to the surface of his skin every once in a while. In the beginning he'd been horrified, but now he found it amazing—if not downright funny—what terrorists chose to put in dirty bombs. Bits of plastic. Hairpins. Parts of paper clips. Anything. Everything.

Some of the parts hurt. Some didn't. Some scarred. Some didn't. Mostly Fox was grateful that nothing had hit his face or eyes—or the cargo below his waist, not that he anticipated having sex again in this century. You had to give a damn about someone to get it up. He didn't. Still, it mattered fiercely to him that his equipment still functioned normally. Go figure.

His obsession with showers, though, had evolved from a terror of infection. He didn't fear dying, but damn, he couldn't face the risk of another hospital stay if any more sores got infected.

When the water turned cool, he flicked off the faucets and reached blind for the towel. He moved carefully, because sometimes his left leg gave out. Technically the broken wrist and thigh bone were both healed, but something inside still wasn't totally kosher, because one minute he could be standing or walking, and the next his left leg would give out.

Tonight that wasn't a problem—but apparently the fates couldn't let him get off scot-free.

The first step out of the shower, he found himself teetering like an old man, dizzy and disoriented. The same child's face swam in front of his eyes, drifting in the foggy steam of the bathroom—real, then not real, clear, then not clear. Sometimes the boy turned into one of the students he'd had; sometimes it was the boy in the dusty yellow alley on the other side of the world. He leaned against the glass shower doors and tried taking a long, slow breath, then another.

A headache was coming. A headache always followed one of the flashbacks to the kid. If he ever got his sense of humor back, he'd think it was funny for a guy, who used to dare anything in life, to be this scared of a headache. Of course, that was then and this was now. Before the pain attacked, he had to get himself out of the bathroom and settled somewhere safer.

Abruptly he heard something…the sound of a door opening? Either he imagined the sound—which would hardly be headline news—or it was Harry, coming to restock the refrigerator with another set of dinners he couldn't eat. Whatever. He leaned over, hands on his knees, waiting for the soupy feeling to pass. Beads of water started drying on his bare skin, chilling him. His hair dripped. The towel…it seemed he'd dropped the towel. He'd get it. In a minute.

"Fergus?"

It was Bear's voice. Ben's, not Harry's. "In here." Damn, he hoped his oldest brother wouldn't stay long. Bear hovered over him like…well, like a bear. All fierce and protective. All angry at anyone and anything who'd hurt him. All willing to do anything to make it all better.

Fox had told his brothers a dozen times that nothing was going to make this all better. The wounds'd heal. They were almost healed now. But whatever was broken inside him seemed like the old Humpty Dumpty story. Too many pieces. Not enough glue.

"Fox?"

He tried denying the dizziness, pushing past it, repeated, "In here."

The denial thing seemed to work. He forced himself to pluck the towel from the tiled floor and straighten before Bear saw him and got the idea again that he was too sick to live alone.

"Hey, Fox, I brought…"

Oops. He'd assumed it'd be his brother standing in the doorway, but his brother was six-three and a solid 220. The intruder had thick, straight, long red hair, almost as long as her waist. Small, classic features. Blue eyes that snapped with attitude, a few freckles on the bridge of a bitsy nose, pale eyebrows arched just so. And a soft, wide mouth.

He remembered that soft, wide mouth. Actually, he remembered every detail of her features. It wasn't that he wanted to remember her, but she was one of those rare women who no guy could possibly forget.

God knew why. She was no angel. That was for damn sure.

Even if her eyes and posture didn't indicate excess attitude, she was wearing a red top again today—a red that screamed next to all that thick red hair. She must have bought the jeans in the boys section, because they bagged at the knees and drooped on her nonexistent butt. Then there were the boots— which were beyond-belief girl shoes and not real boots at all—three striped colors and a high heel. She'd kill herself if she walked far in them.

He caught all of her in a glance. One glance—that no amount of dizziness seemed to blur.

Obviously, finding him in the bathroom doorway had stalled her in midsprint. She'd apparently been heading for the living room, where she'd found him last time. Even if she'd guessed the location of the bathroom, she wouldn't necessarily expect to find anyone standing there, naked as a jaybird.

Her gaze met his, then dropped below his waist, then shot right back up to his eyes faster than lightning.

"Aw, damn. Aw, shoot. Aw, beans," Bear said behind him. "Phoebe, Fox, I'm sorry. Fox, I should have told you I was bringing Phoebe—I never heard the shower, just assumed you were in the living room—"

Fox took his own sweet time, wrapping the towel around his waist. Hell, she'd already seen the main event, and there was no way to hide all the bites and gouges and scars with one lone towel anyway. Besides which, if he tried moving too fast he'd likely end up falling on his nose. "I'll be darned. Did I forget calling for a physical therapist?"

"Now, Fox, you know I brought her. And I told you before, she's not like the other physical therapists you tried. She's more a masseuse."

"Oh, yeah, now I remember that masseuse thing." Fox met her eyes square. "It's okay then, you can go home. That's the one part on my body that I know is still working just fine."

She sighed, but instead of looking insulted—as he'd hoped—she seemed to look amused. "Sex'd probably be the best thing for you, but you're out of luck, I've had no training in that. For the record, I do have a PT license from Duke. And as far as body work, I'm licensed in Deep Tissue, Swedish, Shiatsu, Rolfing, Reflexology, PNF, and NautThai—"

"PNF?"

"Proprioceptive Neuromuscular Facilitation—"

"Forget it. Let's go back to why you've had no training in sex—"

"You're sure feeling peppier today," she announced, which lifted his spirits like nothing else had in ages.

The thing was—if he could fool her, he could fool his brothers. Down the pike, he might even be able to fool himself. In the meantime, she'd itched his curiosity. "Why in hell would you throw out a degree from Duke in physical therapy to do massage work?"

"So I can get my hands on naked men. Why else?"

He saw his brother making frantic hand-motion signs behind her back—Ben was acting increasingly weird. But Fergus couldn't take his eyes off her.

It wasn't that she appealed to him exactly. She couldn't, when no woman was yanking his chain these days—and the kind of woman who always appealed to him had boobs and a butt. She had neither, but damn. She was just so…zesty. Who'd have guessed she'd laugh when he tried to insult her?

Obviously, he had to try harder to annoy her.

"I'd think you could get your hands on a lot of naked men without having to bother guys who aren't interested."

"You're so right. Getting men naked is amazingly easy. On the other hand, easy guys never turned me on. I like a challenge."

"A challenge to you is barreling into a guy's house who never asked you?"

She should have bristled for that one at least. Defended herself. Fought back. Instead she just said, "Not usually. But I'm making an exception because you're so darn adorable that I'd probably break all the rules to get my hands on you. What can I say? You really ring my chimes, cutie."

That was such an outright fib that she darn near rendered him speechless. His eyes narrowed. Nobody, but nobody, rendered him speechless. "You're so full of bologna, I can't believe it."

"What makes you think I'm full of bologna?"

"Because you're not remotely promiscuous." God knew how such a personal comment flew out of his mouth, except it somehow bugged him, her talking about all those naked men. In spite of that luscious mouth and her wearing those absurdly sexy high boots, she just didn't come across to him as easy—not any kind of easy. Beneath that whole frisky act, there was just something vulnerable about her.

Once the comment came out of his mouth, though, he had

no chance to take it back. Her hands immediately formed small fists and arched on her hips. "How do you know I'm not promiscuous?"

"All right, all right, of course I don't *know* it. I don't know you from Adam. But twenty bucks on the table says you've been celibate for the last year." *There.* It was gone faster than a flash, but for that quarter of a millisecond he caught something in her eyes. Never mind the big talk and the long, gorgeous hair and all that sensuality reeking from her. She *had* been celibate.

"For all you know," she said, "I'm happily married and have been having sex three times a day with my darling."

"Yeah? So, are you married?"

She rolled her eyes with exasperation. "No, I'm not married—but for all you know I sleep with ten men a week—not that it matters either way. How on earth did we wander so far from the point? And the point, Fox, is whether you would or wouldn't like another head rub. You've got another bad headache coming on, don't you."

Hell. He not only had a bad headache coming on; the buildup felt like the mother of all earthquakes warming up in his skull. But for an instant he'd almost forgotten. He'd almost forgotten his head, his injuries, his depression. That he was standing there naked except for a towel. That his brother was right behind her. That the life he'd once known seemed to have clicked its heels and taken off for Kansas, because he didn't recognize himself or his life anymore.

She'd distracted him. Something about her seemed to reach in him like no one else had in a blue moon—and it shook him up good. He dropped the teasing tone and said quietly, "You're right. I've got another headache coming on. But

I don't need anyone's help to handle it." And without skip-ping a beat he turned to his brother. "Bear, leave her *alone.*"

He wasn't exactly sure where that directive came from, ex-cept that both his brothers seemed unusually taken with Phoebe—not that he cared. But he just kept getting some in-stinct that she wasn't as tough and full of pepper as she let on. On that first night she'd said something like, "Fox, I'm nobody. Nobody you need to worry about"—as if she thought of herself as no one consequential—and it had gnawed in his memory ever since. How ridiculous was that?

Hell, the thought that she needed protecting—that he could even consider himself a protector—boggled his mind. And his mind was already too damned shredded to need any more boggling.

Without another word he stalked down the hall to his bed-room, where he firmly closed the door. There was no lock, but there didn't need to be.

No one called after him. No one tried to get in. He figured his rudeness got through…which was exactly what needed to happen. Fergus knew his brothers meant well. He knew his brothers were trying to help him—including their bringing in that little redhead.

He didn't mean to—or like—taking his surliness out on her, but something about Phoebe really bugged him. Really, really got to him. The problem was weird and unsettling…but not complicated.

All he had to do was stay away from her. Piece of cake.

Phoebe barely glanced up at the rap on her door. Saturday mornings half the neighborhood popped over—a tradition she'd started when she first moved here, stemming from a trick her mom had taught her. She set a fresh-baked almond cinnamon coffee cake on the porch to cool.

That was it. The whole trick. Even the meanest neighbor or the shyest stranger couldn't seem to resist the smell. Which was all well and good, but usually the group waited until eight before showing up. Her hair was still down, her feet still bare, her terry cloth shorts and tee on the ragged side of decent, when Gary stuck his head in.

"Hey, Phoebe."

"Hey, you. Mary still sleeping in?"

"Yeah. It was the same when she was pregnant before. Sleeps like the dead." He ambled over, plucked a fresh piece of coffee cake, no plate, no napkin, and then chose a place to sprawl. Her other neighbor, Fred, had already settled at the head of the table. Traditionally he galloped over with his walker at the first smell coming out of the oven.

"You're going to burn your fingers," she warned Gary.

"And this is news how?" The mutts immediately took root on laps—one on Fred's, one on Gary's.

Phoebe poured the boys coffee, but then went back to the counter where she was slicing a grapefruit. Her cooking specialty was the almond cinnamon coffee cake—and not that she was bragging, but it was even better than her mother's, and her mom's was the best in the universe. Unfortunately and ironically, she seemed to be a grapefruit addict herself—for which the neighbors teased her mercilessly.

The back door whooshed open again. "Hi, sweetie," Barb greeted her. Within seconds she was battling with Gary for the coffee cake spatula. "Give it. My God, you guys already leveled a coffee cake on your own. How could you be so greedy?"

Phoebe ignored the fight and concentrated on her grapefruit. Her neighbors, thank God, could take anyone's mind off their troubles. It was the first time in days she hadn't thought about Fergus.

Barb seemed to relish the role of the neighborhood bawd. Even this early on a Saturday, she was wearing a low-dipping top, slick spandex pants, and a full arsenal of makeup. She'd been married to a plastic surgeon. It showed.

"So what's new around here?" Barbara won the coffee cake piece she wanted, sashayed over to the coffee and then went prowling down the hall carrying her cup.

"Nothing," Phoebe answered.

"Oh, yes, there is. I'll find it. You're always doing something new around here." A moment later Barbara called back, "I'll be damned. You cleaned."

"I did not." Phoebe was offended she'd been accused of such a thing.

"You did. There's no dust."

She'd only cleaned because she was worried about that damned man. That wasn't the same as compulsive cleaning, now, was it? It was just something to do at two in the morning when she was pacing around, fretting whether that rockheaded jerk was in pain and alone. Before she could invent a respectable reason for the lack of mess and dust, though, Barbara let out a shriek from far down the hall.

"Oh, my God, what kind of gigantic construction project have you got going on in here?"

"What, what?" That got both Fred and Gary out of their chairs, Fred leading the charge with his walker through the house.

Phoebe sighed mightily and traipsed after them. It confounded her how such a private person—such as herself—

could end up with such nosy neighbors. They seemed end-lessly fascinated by everything she did to the house, partly because they thought she was unconventional and artistic.

That was hooey. Reality was that she'd only bought the house because she couldn't find a rental that worked for her setup, and the only house she could swing had to be a major fixer-upper. The location was unbeatable, three blocks off Main Street, so it was an easy walk for customers. The structure was a basic two-story saltbox built in the sixties. There were balconies on both floors and no termites—those were the positives.

Then came the fixer-upper part. The windows hadn't been caulked in a decade; the drive could have starred in a jungle movie, and the yard resembled a wildlife sanctuary. When she tried selling her neighbors the sanctuary theory, though, someone loaned her a lawn mower. Pretty clear what the neighborhood standard was, and weedy wasn't it.

The neighbors were more fascinated by what she did with the inside. From the beginning she realized the house was going to suck in millions to make it habitable—only she didn't have millions. Cripes, she didn't even have furniture. So she'd headed for Home Depot and bought paint. Lots of paint.

The kitchen cabinets were mint green, the walls a bright blue. Beyond the kitchen was a dining room she'd turned into an office, and painted those walls a light lavender. An arched doorway led into a long narrow vanilla-yellow living room. All in all, the downstairs pretty much covered every possible ice cream cone color.

In some rooms, she even had furniture now.

In the back of the house, where Barb hustled the breakfasters, was her business. Customers—usually moms—entered from the back door.

A bathroom and curtained-off changing area took up the north wall; the massage center dominated the room's center. The counters, sink, stand-alone tub and massage tables were all white—not shiny, in-your-face white, but an ultra-soft clean white.

All, that is, except for one corner, where dusty bags of cement, heaped stacks of stones and long boxes of plumbing parts looked as out of place as mud in a hospital. Further, the sledgehammer in front of it at all was almost bigger than she was. She may have overbought there, just a tad.

"What in God's name have you gotten yourself into, girl?" Gary questioned, hands on hips.

Phoebe was still carrying her bowl of grapefruit. It was impossible to explain that once she'd cleaned the place stem to stern—even the windows—she still couldn't get her mind off the damn man. He was hurting, she just knew it. Not letting anyone help him, she knew that, too. But it wasn't her problem—and wasn't going to be her problem—so she'd searched for a project that would force her to think about something else.

"I'm going to build a waterfall," she told the group.

"A waterfall," Barb repeated. "Honey, you barely have a pot to pee in, and you give away half of what you do have. And you're going to build a waterfall? Inside the house?"

"Now wait. Just wait. It's not as impossible as it sounds. I saw it in a magazine…" And then she mentally pictured it. The south corner of this room really had nothing in it, so there's where she wanted it—a sensual, warm, indoor waterfall at shower height, leading to a small pool surrounded by tropical plants. "If I used tile inside, stone outside, it would look almost like the real thing. And I could use it with the babies, either by sitting in there by myself, or just have the parent sit with their little one. It wouldn't be too different from a hot tub, just more…sensual. And natural. And restful."

Gary and Fred took one look at the bags of cement and piles of stones and started guffawing.

"Hey. It can't be that hard to find a mason who can show me how to mortar in the stones. And I figured the pipes for the sink are already here, so there has to be some way to tap into them for the water source. I mean, I know it'll take some work—"

"Some work?" Gary hooted. "You're going to need a crew of fifty to pull this off!"

"So, it'll take a lot of work. But I really think it's a practical idea—" Since that sent Gary and Barb into new gales of laughter, she appealed to Fred. "Don't you think it'd be beautiful?"

"I think you're the prettiest thing this neighborhood has seen in decades, sugar. And if you want to build yourself a waterfall, then that's what you should do."

But then he caught Gary's eye, and the two of them started cackling all over again.

At that precise moment she spotted the man in the doorway—not *any* man, but Fergus. Her Fergus Lockwood. He had his arm raised in a fist, as if he'd been knocking and was going to try yet again to gain someone's attention.

The pups spotted him first and beelined straight for the newcomer. Her neighbors all spun around and gaped, then gaped back at Phoebe, then offered hellos and we're just

Phoebe's neighbors and everybody was just leaving—although no one left.

Phoebe dropped her bowl of grapefruit. The bowl cracked. The grapefruit skittered across the tile floor, leaving seeds and grapefruit juice in its wake. Obviously the world as she knew it hadn't suddenly ended, yet, for just a few seconds she couldn't seem to move. Her heart went woosh, the way it had a nasty tendency to do around Fox the other two times she'd been near him—only it was worse this time.

It was all his fault she'd come up with this ridiculously impossible waterfall idea. All his fault she'd cleaned house. It was the woosh thing. His brothers were adorable, so at least if they caused that thigh-clenching heart-thumping response, she'd have understood it. She recognized those guys as hot, but not a problem.

Why did she only feel that woosh and zing for the wrong guys? And, darn it, one short glance at his long, lean bones and her hormones were all a dazzle. Where was the fairness in life? The justice?

"Phoebe? I didn't mean to barge in, but the bell didn't seem to work, and no one seemed to hear me knocking. When I heard all the voices, I—"

"It's okay," she said swiftly, and zoomed forward—almost putting her bare foot in the broken porcelain but getting smart at the last second. A little smart, anyway. "These are my neighbors—Barb, Gary, Fred, this is Fergus—"

"We're leaving," Barb said again, as she pumped his hand. Fergus went rigid.

Phoebe saw his response and recognized that he was hurting. Thankfully that slapped a little sense in her head. "Y'all can take the rest of the coffee cake on your way out. And I'll catch up with you later," she said firmly.

It took a minute to clear them out, clean up the broken bowl, have a heart attack because she'd had no chance to brush her hair or put on makeup or real clothes, get Mop and Duster to quit behaving like puppies on speed, and then get back to him.

He was still standing exactly where she'd left him, looking around her massage room setup. "Phoebe, I really am sorry about interrupting you."

"You didn't. That was just a Saturday-morning neighborhood free-for-all. They eat me out of house and home. What's wrong?"

He answered her slowly, quietly, his gaze directly on hers. "I was rude before. I wanted to apologize. When I go through one of my bad pain stretches, I can't seem to…think. My foot was so deep in my mouth, I'm amazed I could even get it out again. I'm sorry if I hurt your feelings."

"You didn't. And it's not a worry. I understand about pain." She cocked her head curiously. "But you could have called to say you were sorry. Instead…you're here."

He tugged on an ear. "Yeah, well. Nothing I tried ever helped those headaches. You did. And if you'd consider taking me and my sometimes big mouth on as a client, I'd appreciate it."

He obviously hated eating crow. She couldn't very well hold a grudge when she hated sucking up after making a mistake herself. "I take it you're having one of those headaches right now?"

"I've got one coming," he admitted. "But that's not why I came now. The headache isn't that bad. And I didn't expect you'd be working on Saturdays. I just came to apologize, and I figured Saturday morning you might not have clients, so it'd be a good time to ask if you'd consider taking me on down the pike—"

Before he could finish, she said, "All right."

"All right, you'll take me on?"

"Yes. If we can come to terms." She perched up on a counter and crossed her bare feet. "If you want me to work with you, Fergus, my idea would be to sit down together with a whole program. Not just deal with those headaches when they're tearing you in two, because that timing is way too late. You need to practice some techniques to make them go away for the long term."

"Like what techniques? What kind of program?" he asked warily, but her attention was diverted when she saw him starting to sway.

"Strip down," she said swiftly.

"Beg your pardon?"

"You're on my turf now, Fox. Go behind the curtain, strip down—I don't care if you keep on your underwear or go buff—but take off most of your clothes. I need two minutes to heat the sheet and prepare. When you're done, come back in here, get on the table, cover up."

"I—"

"Do it," she ordered him.

She wasn't going to think about it—about how or why he rang her chimes. Or about that stupid euphoric feeling she got around him, either.

It had cost him to come here, particularly for a man who had a hard time leaving the house these days. And though he may not have been in serious pain when he started out, he was obviously getting more miserable by the minute. She kicked her speed up to high gear. The pups were sent outside, the phone put on no-ring. The massage table was automatically dressed with a clean white pad, but it was baby-size. She scouted out an adult one, then threw a sheet in the dryer to heat on high for a few minutes.

Minutes before, she'd worried about looking like something a cat wouldn't drag home, but any thought of vanity disappeared now. Impatiently she pushed up her long hair, twisting and clipping it, while she considered which oils she wanted. She decided on lemon balm, sweet marjoram and calendula. She clicked on the CD, then strategically placed several small towels where they'd cushion his neck, the small of his back, under his knees.

She heard him cough—and easily guessed he was on the other side of the dressing room curtain, ready, just not sure what to do next. She didn't look up, just said, "Climb on the table and lie down on your back. I'm going to pull the shades, darken the room so it won't be so bright, Fox. There's a cover you can pull on, if you're too cool."

She used her bossiest voice, yet she still momentarily held her breath, unsure if he'd try giving her a hard time. But he said nothing. Once he settled on the table, she turned around and immediately smoothed a cool compress on his forehead and eyes until she finished setting up. On the CD player she clicked on madrigals. She'd never liked that kind of music, but this wasn't about her. Somehow even the most rowdiest babies seem to quiet down when she used that disc.

The details were done, then, and once she moved behind his head, she concentrated as fiercely as a brain surgeon. This was work. It wasn't about *him;* it wasn't about sex; it wasn't about analyzing why such a scrawny, stubborn, contrary man put such an impossible zing in her pulse.

It was just about a man who was hurting…and about her, hoping to find a way to help him.

She worked for fifteen solid minutes, but his headache was almost as stubborn as he was. He just couldn't seem to relax. The pain had a grip on him with wolf teeth. She leaned forward, closing her eyes, feeling his heartbeat, feeling the heat of his skin, feeling his pain…and then going for it. Temples. Eyes. Frontal lobe. The sides of his neck, under his chin, his whole face. Then into his scalp.

Two minutes passed. Then five. Seven more minutes passed before he even started letting go…but then he was hers. Her heart suddenly quickened with a rhythm she couldn't shake. She never got that feeling with her babies. Never got it with her elderly clients. Touch was sensual and healing and fulfilling, and she needed—liked—to help people. But it wasn't sexual.

It was so, so sexual with him. Intuiting where to touch, how to move, wasn't just about evaluating his pain. It was about sensing what he wanted. What he liked. What moved him.

Even though the pain finally eased, he didn't open his eyes for a long time. Silently she pulled up the sides on the massage table so he wouldn't accidentally fall, but still she stood there, knowing he wasn't totally asleep yet. His body fought sleep, naturally wary that if he let go completely, the pain could steal up on him again.

At one point he murmured, "I just want you to know…I'm not marrying anyone. But if I were…it'd be you."

"Yeah, yeah, that's what all the guys say," she quipped easily, but her voice was still a careful whisper.

He fell silent again, but not for long enough. "I almost forgot. You warned me before about all those men you have in your life."

She hadn't warned him. She'd just said what he was undoubtedly already thinking because of her being a masseuse, but she let it go. Seconds ticked by. Then minutes. Finally his breathing turned deep and even. She watched his chest rise and fall, watched the thick furrow between his brows smooth out, watched those tightly muscled shoulders finally ease completely.

The idle thought sneaked into her mind that this had to be the craziest thing that had ever happened to her. The guy hadn't touched her. In any way. She was the only one who'd done the touching. Yet she was somehow more drawn to him than any other man she could remember.

It was downright scary having to worry that she was losing her mind this young.

And it was scarier yet to realize that this fierce, wonderful pull she had for Fox was so dead wrong. He was a man whose wealth and background was bound to make him look down on her and her profession, a man who had shown no interest in her. A man as inappropriate for her as Alan had been. A man who had the potential to hurt her, she feared, even deeper than Alan had.

Four

The dream stirred Fox into waking. In the dream a sizzling-hot sun fried his back—just like every other day. For months he'd wondered if that incessant sun had ever driven anyone mad. Yet he wanted to be here. Wanted to do this.

The last few days, they'd been clearing debris, starting the work of rebuilding a school. It was more than good work. It was exactly the reason he'd felt driven to enlist. Back home the honor thing had bugged him. He couldn't teach kids history every day and discuss what it took to be a hero and an American without realizing that it was damn well time for him to actively show instead of tell. The other reason was the kids. Having the chance to rebuild hospitals and schools made him believe that his kids, his students, just might have a better world to grow up in.

And that was exactly why he didn't hesitate to crouch

down when the little brown-faced squirt shyly approached him. He offered the tyke some candy, a yoyo. He knew the language, which was partly why he'd ended up there. And the child with the big brown eyes and hollow cheeks looked hungry and desperate, as if somehow, some way, somebody had to do something to make his life better.

That the child had a bomb wrapped around his belly never crossed his mind. Never. Not for a second. Not even when it went off…and he was blown back a dozen yards, scissors and shards of God knows what spearing every surface on his body that wasn't covered by gear. And the kid, that damn kid, that damn damn damn baby of a kid…

And that's when Fox woke up. When he always woke up. But this time he was as disoriented as a priest in a brothel.

Something was really, really screwy.

This wasn't the leather couch where he always fell asleep. Instead he seemed to be lying on some kind of cushioned surface, wrapped in a soft warm sheet. Everything around him was saint white, except for a bunch of bosomy plants hanging in windows, spilling leaves and flowers in crowded tangles. For some goofy reason there was a bathtub in the middle of the room, and yet the far corner was heaped with stones and construction and plumbing parts. Goofier yet, his nostrils picked up the most wonderful smells—the sharp tang of lemon and a minty herb fragrance, and then another scent, something he couldn't quite identify, something vague and fresh and brisk and just a bit flowery.…

Her.

The minute he turned his head, he saw Phoebe. As always when he woke after a crash-deep, crash-dark sleep, the head ache was completely gone and his senses ultrasharp. He could feel every ache, every fading stitch and bruise.

He also promptly realized that he was naked as a jaybird under the sheet—and hard as a jackhammer. One look at her seemed to do it.

She was curled up in a white rocker. All the blinds in the room were drawn, except where she'd opened them several inches in the south window above her. Sunshine beamed down—as if just for her. Her bare legs were swung over the chair arm, and the shape of her naked calves was enough to inspire another jolt of testosterone. Her bare feet were dirty, and she was wearing what he called Saturday clothes, sweats, shorts and a big old voluminous shirt that completely concealed her body.

She held a mug of something steaming in one hand, a book in the other. He vaguely remembered her hair all pinned up and out of the way, but she'd let it loose at some point, because now those long red strands shimmied down her back like a gush of water, catching claret and cinnamon and tea and amber colors in the sunlight. The freckles on her nose were naked.

He wished she were.

He'd never met a more sensual woman. In looks, in touch, in everything. He felt both defensive and suspicious about that weird magic thing when she touched him. He just didn't get it…how she could possibly induce so much feeling in a guy who *didn't* feel, didn't talk, had cut himself off from life for months now—and wanted it that way.

But none of that aggravation seemed to dent his fascination for her. Fox conceded that the issue might be a lot simpler than he was making it. Probably any man'd have to be dead not to respond to a two hundred percent handful of a woman like her.

She startled, as if suddenly realizing something was different in the room. When she turned her head and saw he was awake, she immediately plunked down her mug.

"What time is it?" he asked her.

"Almost three."

Couldn't be. "You're *not* telling me I've been here all day."

"You were sleeping so soundly that I didn't want to wake you. And there was no need. I was just puttering around here. No clients on a Saturday."

"I'll pay you for the time I was here."

"Yeah, you will," she agreed. "But if you feel up to it, I'd like to ask you some questions." She pushed out of the rocking chair, came closer.

"What kind of questions?" he asked suspiciously.

"A massage shouldn't be able to dent the kind of serious headaches you're getting, Fergus. Migraines and cluster headaches and stuff that bad…they're medical. Physiological."

"Yeah, so I've been told." She was close enough to see the tent in the sheet, but she seemed to be looking straight in his eyes. He willed the mountain to wilt, but damned if it didn't seem to be getting harder instead of softer.

"It just doesn't make sense. That I've been able to help you with headaches as bad as you get them. Do you have any idea at all about what brings them on?"

He closed his eyes, opened them again. "The docs said, after ruling out a bunch of medical reasons, that the headaches had to be some kind of stress response."

"Stress I can work with you on."

"Work with me," he echoed.

"I mentioned it earlier. I'll work up a program, then send it over to you and your family, so you can look at it on your own time, see if you're willing to give it a shot. The thing is, what we're doing now is shutting the barn door after the horse is already loose. Trying to beat pain when it's already sucked you under is like trying to reason with an enemy who's already won. What you want, ideally, is to get power over the pain ahead of time. Before it's gotten bad."

"Okay. Makes sense." He was unsure why she sounded so tentative and wary. He hadn't been very nice to her, no. But there was something in her voice, her face, as if she were braced for him to dismiss anything she said.

Again she said carefully, "That's all I can really do. Teach you some techniques to work with stress and pain. I can also give you some strength- and stamina-building exercises, both to help give you some ammunition against the pain and to help you sleep better."

"That's a joke. I don't sleep." He also wasn't usually this chatty, but damn it, the more she looked at him with those big, soft, blue eyes, the more his hormones felt giddy with wonder. Goofy, but there it was.

To slap some reality into his head, he tried to move. She didn't leap to help him, just watched him struggle to push himself into a sitting position. It took forever, which royally ticked him off. He'd had it with the recovery business in every way. Eventually, keeping the sheet bunched around his waist, he managed to angle his long hairy legs over the side and sit up straight.

"Fox," she said quietly, "could you give me a bigger picture here? Your life isn't my business, I realize, but it'd still help if I understood more about what you normally do, what you want to do. Your brothers filled me in a little. They said that you left a full-time job to join the military. That you got a military discharge from the service—so that's off the table now. That you're only temporarily living in the bachelor house, close to family, until you're fully recovered."

"So far you're dealing aces."

"Okay, but what's the rest of the story? Are you planning on living in Gold River long-term? Planning on going back to work soon, and if so, what kind of work? What kind of physical activities or hobbies do you normally do or want to do?"

He scraped a hand through his hair. There was a smell on his skin, in his hair, all around him. A softness. That lemon balm scent thing. It wasn't exactly girly, but it sure as hell didn't go with hairy legs and a torso full of jagged scars.

"Before I joined the service, I was a teacher. A history teacher." At her look of surprise, he said, "Yeah, I get that same look from everyone. My brothers chose businesses that make money hand over fist, and somehow I elected for the do-gooder career. Anyway. I taught middle school. The hellion ages, when the kids are all dripping hormones and getting big mouths and give their teachers grief nonstop. Teaching was kind of like juggling dynamite every day. Probably why it appealed."

"So…are you hoping to go back to teaching this fall?"

"I'm never going back to teaching," he said curtly. "Do you answer questions, too, or just ask them?"

She blinked. "What do you want to know?"

"How you happen to be living in Gold River."

"I'd been doing physical therapy work for a hospital. I liked the work, but there came a point when I wanted to concentrate on babies—and I wanted to work independently, make my own business. So I started the *Baby Love* massage thing. And I just like it here. The town, the people, everything."

"Originally you came from—?"

"Asheville."

"And where's the guy in this picture?"

"What guy?"

"That's what I'm asking. You left Asheville for a small town like this, there was a guy involved," he said with certainty.

"Okay," she said cheerfully, and whipped around. "You're obviously feeling better. I've got groceries to buy, dogs to run, and I'm going to the movies with friends tonight. So, I'll let you get dressed in some privacy so you can take off. I'll drop a program plan at your place. Then you can call if you decide it's something you want to do...."

He didn't know he was going to do it. Ease off the table, twist the sheet around his waist toga fashion and go after her. It wasn't as if she charged out of the room at gallop speed. He easily caught up with her by the hall, looped his hand around her wrist.

She startled at the contact, turned her head.

Fox was aggravated at that moment. It wasn't a rational feeling, just an awareness that something was...out of kilter. She gave off heavy, warm caring vibes one second...and bristly defensiveness the next. She wasn't his problem, so her being confusing shouldn't matter. But it did. Somehow it did. There was something building between them...like ashes that could turn into white-hot coals if they were stirred.

He couldn't pin down his own intentions. Somewhere, though, he'd started worrying that she had feelings for him. Sexual feelings. Real feelings. And that couldn't be, because for now and the whole indefinite future he was in no shape to care for anyone. So maybe he intended on scaring her. Or annoying her. Hell, who knew? He hadn't had a functioning brain in a blue moon.

He just knew when he touched her arm, when she whipped toward him, when he saw the look in her eyes…that he was going to kiss her.

That she knew a kiss was coming.

And then…

Then he just did it.

Took that soft, crushable, sexy mouth.

Who could guess he'd set off an explosion? Maybe she hadn't been kissed in a while. Maybe her body was going through some kind of hormone overdrive. Maybe she really did like him—well, that last theory didn't seem likely. The Lockwood men used to be women magnets, himself included, but he'd thrown out any ability to charm when he'd taken on a body full of scars.

But damn.

She *did* seem to be igniting for him, even if he couldn't explain it.

Her skillful, sensual hands slid up, looped around his neck, clung. That mouth molded under his, melted under his, moved under his, communicating yearning and longing. Communicating desire. Her tongue suddenly whispered against his. Her soft, full breasts suddenly ached against his chest. Her throat suddenly let out a sweet bleat of helplessness.

The sheet wrapped around his waist gave up fighting gravity and fell to the floor in a woosh. He knew he'd never manage to stand upright long—not just because his injured leg lacked strength—but because all the oxygen in his head had dropped heavier than thunder to below his waist.

His hands framed her face, holding her still as he grappled to understand how a single kiss could become Armageddon. He tried another kiss to find out, since the first one only raised giant-size questions and answered absolutely none. After that he took her mouth a third time, his reasons getting fuzzier. But the silky soft exploration of her lips and tongue and teeth seemed totally necessary. It wasn't that he was looking for trouble...

His conscience nicked him for the fib. All right, all right, he was looking for a *little* trouble. He'd righteously ducked away from thinking about women since his injuries, telling himself that love—and sex—simply had to be taken off his table indefinitely. How was he supposed to know that deprivation had been haunting him? Or that he'd been *damn* worried about whether his body was still able to function normally.

It was.

Charlie, let loose, wagged around like a happy puppy tail, poking and pressing against her abdomen with uninhibited enthusiasm. Phoebe was short. Impossibly short. If he'd just had the strength, he could have lifted her, but as it was, his body creaked and groaned the longer he leaned down, crunching his neck, his spine.

The pain nagged at him, but only like a pesky mosquito. Tasting her, touching her, sipping her, made him feel like a man who was offered a drink of cool, clear water after weeks in the desert. She was so like water, liquid, flowing around him, her kisses drowning the drumbeat in his ears, his head. He immersed himself.

There was no wasting time dipping his foot in the water to test the temperature. He dove straight in, all of him engaged, mouth, elbows, brain, heart—and for damn sure, Charlie. It wasn't as if he were the only one acting insane.

She kissed him back and kept kissing him back. Her throat kept making those yearning, lonesome sounds. Her breasts kept tightening, swaying toward him, into him. Her soft hands held on as if she'd fall if he let her go.

Okay. Fox finally got it. What the deal was.

She wasn't real. She wasn't normal. She was a witch. A conjurer of men's fantasies. Real women just didn't respond to a guy like this—as if she wanted him to do anything he wanted, as if all her inhibitions blew away when he touched her, as if he were the hottest, sexiest guy ever born. As if she'd never lived until he touched her.

Fox remembered that whole fantasy from when he was sixteen. That's how he daydreamed it'd be with a girl—but then of course he grew up. Real women took manners. Real women took finesse and care to ignite. They had to know a guy before they could trust him, and it took serious trust for sex to be good. Well—any sex was better than no sex. But the best stuff was worth taking the time to do right.

With her it was as if someone had created her only for him. She knew just how to taste. Just how to sound. Just how to touch to make his world go dizzy and his mind go daft.

It was so weird. He'd been weak as a kitten for months, yet suddenly he felt powerful enough to move a couple of mountains. For a long, black time, he'd shut off emotion, yet this damned impossible redhead had him thinking about love again. About waking up next to somebody. About being able to weave his fingers through that, long, long silky red hair every night, any night.

"Hey."

It seemed to be his voice, coming out thicker than molasses, interrupting them. Not hers. He lifted his head. She didn't lift hers. He was the one stuck doing the honorable thing and in-serting a little sanity into this madness. Where the Sam Hill was her common sense? She was giving him five million *yes* sig-nals. It was the middle of a Saturday afternoon, for Pete's sake. Her dogs were sitting there with cocked heads as if they were trying to comprehend the totally strange behavior of the humans. The sun was beating in like a benediction. He was hurting. And God knew, pain wasn't new, but he hadn't experienced hurt com-ing from massive sexual frustration until two minutes ago.

"What's going on here?" he demanded lowly.

"Huh? Weren't you the one who suddenly came on to me?"

"But you didn't stop me."

"Like that makes you less guilty for starting this?"

"No. It just makes me completely confused about why you let me kiss you. And why you kissed me back." He couldn't take his eyes off her. Her cheeks were punched with color, her eyes hectic bright. Her hair had been tumbled before, but man, now he'd really made a wreck.

Had she been this breathtaking the first time he'd met her? How come he hadn't noticed it then?

She averted her eyes. "Fox...I feel bad for you. You've been through so much. And you're still going through a lot of pain."

"Ah...so the only reason you kissed me back is because you felt sorry for me?"

She wrapped her arms under her chest, tight. "I know…no guy wants to think that a woman pities him."

"You've got that right."

"But *pity* isn't the right word, Fergus…it's more like compassion."

"So this is all about compassion?" Fox wondered if she'd ever considered selling heaters in the Amazon.

She gave a little laugh. "Okay. There was more to it than that. I'll let you in on a problem I have."

"Sure."

"Guys often seem to think that I'm really into sex because I'm a masseuse. For me, that's been a real conundrum. Obviously, I care about people or I wouldn't have chosen this line of work. But when I touch someone as a masseuse—like I have been with you—it really is about compassion and nothing else. There's no sexual component at all."

Fox struggled to get his mind completely off Charlie. He sensed she was trying to tell him something serious, something critically important, but it was hard to concentrate past his hammering need and her handing out this total nonsense. "I'm not sure what you mean here. Are you saying that you didn't feel anything sexual?"

"It's not personal," she assured him. "I'm just trying to be honest. I'm just not a very sexual person. I'm more maternal, I guess."

"Maternal," he echoed.

She nodded vigorously. "Which is why I work with babies."

"Because you're maternal but not sexual."

"Exactly," she said.

* * *

Wednesday evening Fox still couldn't get that conversation out of his mind. He picked up a glass of water, yet quickly forgot to drink, forgot the buzz of his brothers' conversation in the next room, forgot the homemade lasagna steaming as his mom lifted it from the oven.

What on earth had Phoebe been trying to sell him? That she didn't like sex? That she wasn't a sexual being? That she was just into compassion? Was he supposed to just nod his head and say, oh, sure, horses fly?

Memories kept swirling back. Except for mouth-to-mouth kisses, he'd barely touched her in any intimate way…yet he felt as if he had. And even though he'd been stark naked, she'd only physically touched him above the neck—yet she seemed to touch every emotional chord and hormone he'd ever owned.

So.

He'd already figured out that she was a frightening woman. Unsettling. Unnerving. Unfathomable.

But unsexy?

How could Phoebe conceivably believe that about herself? Why would she want to?

"Fergus, would you pay attention," his mother said irritably.

Fox mentally jerked himself awake, but still knew that this was a precise measure of what a mess that woman had made of him. His mother was right here, carrying her world-famous lasagna, and yet all he could think about was sex and Phoebe.

That was power.

No wonder he was scared of her.

"I was listening," he assured his mother. His brothers loped into the kitchen, undoubtedly driven by the same addictive smell of the gourmet dish.

"I was just trying to tell your youngest brother," his mother said to Bear and Moose, "that people with means simply don't teach school. And since he doesn't seem inclined to teach again, this is an ideal opportunity to reconsider other career choices."

"Okay," Fox said patiently, "what is it you think would be a better career than teaching?"

His mom's eyes lit up, thrilled to be asked. Bear and Moose took the far chairs and slunk down low and quiet. They'd been in the hot seat. They didn't like it. It didn't get better with age. "Something that involves making serious money. And more participation in the community."

"Well, actually, Mom, I make a ton of money. I've been investing for years." Fox shot his brothers a look. How fast the traitors dove into the lasagna. Next time *you* need help, I'll be in Tahiti. "And as far as participating in the community, I'm working directly with kids. Or I was. How else could I possibly participate more productively?"

"You could be a senator," his mother said firmly.

"You would wish that on me? A life in politics?" He added, *"No."*

"Well then…if you haven't got any other plans on the burner, *are* you thinking about teaching this coming fall? As far as I know you still have an active contract, don't you?"

God, she was sly. Other moms were, well, sweet. His was trickier than a con artist. She wanted him to rejoin life again. She wanted him to care about work and life and himself again. Except that even for his mother—and God knew he loved her—he couldn't imagine going back into a classroom.

When he failed to answer, Georgia Lockwood pounced on the reason they were all together. "Furthermore, you haven't told me anything about this woman Bear and Moose keep talking about. I don't understand why she's coming here, and I don't understand why you're involved with her."

"She didn't have to come here. She just offered to explain the whole program thing to the family. And I'm not involved with her."

His mother looked at him over the top of her delicate gold-wire rims. "Fergus, don't think I just fell off the turnip truck."

Neither brother, on the other side of the table, even breathed. They just kept shoveling in the lasagna. "Trust me, Mom. I never thought that."

"A masseuse." Georgia rolled her eyes. "Come *on*. I realize that you're an unmarried man, that you have…needs. People don't wait like they used to. I may not agree with how things have changed, but I can at least understand it. I would be perfectly happy to hear you have a young woman in your life on *any* basis."

"Mom—"

"I won't be judgmental. You don't have to ever worry about that."

"Mom—"

"I would like grandchildren. I admit it. None of you seems to be moving in that direction. I blame your father for making you all so independent and…rowdy." She sighed. "But never mind that. The point is in principle, I'd prefer grandchildren coming from a two-parent family and our last name—"

"Mom!"

"—however, if there's no other way I can get them, you can just bring them home in whatever form they come. I won't say a word. Not a word."

Fergus shot his brothers a look that would have fried an ice cube. They'd blackmailed him into this whole deal—setting him up with Phoebe, then conning him into being there when Phoebe presented this program thing. And now where were they? Taking in mom's lasagna like vultures but not helping him worth beans. "Mom, get it out of your head. She's *not* a date. Not anyone I'm seeing that way—"

Precisely at that moment they all whipped around at a knock on the door. And there was Phoebe—who'd obviously poked in her head when she couldn't rouse anyone's attention any other way. When she stepped in, shock numbed his tongue. She looked nine months pregnant.

A second later, of course, he realized that it wasn't her stomach, but something *on* her stomach making that huge lump. A baby. A real live baby. All swaddled in some kind of papoose carrier that was strapped to her tummy.

Fox recovered his breath and started to stand up and greet her, but never had the chance. His mother took one look at the baby and surged toward Phoebe like a human tidal wave, her eyes suddenly brighter than diamonds. "Well, you obviously have to be Phoebe! You didn't tell me she liked babies, Fox. Isn't that nice? Come right on in, dear, and I'll get you a plate. I'm Mrs. Lockwood, but you feel free to call me Georgia. If you don't want lasagna, could I talk you into some coffee or sweet tea? I was just telling the boys, how wonderful it was that you'd involved Fergus's whole family in this, um, program…"

Fox took one look at Phoebe's face and felt his heart sink. Her friendly smile looked forced and frozen. She must have heard what he said—about not being a date, not being anyone he was seeing. She'd probably even heard the deprecating comment his mom had said about masseuses. Hell and double hell. She had no way of knowing that he'd just been trying to divert his mother from giving her the third degree…and now, she ignored him completely as she walked in. She greeted his mother and then crossed the room to give each of his brothers a kiss.

His brothers.

Both of them.

Got the kisses.

Not him. She ignored him as if he were a puppy puddle.

"Why, no one told me you were bringing a baby, dear." Her mom descended on Phoebe as if a long-lost relative had suddenly shown up. So much for a prejudice against masseuses. Put a baby in the picture, and Georgia was now happy to treat Phoebe like a goddess.

"Actually, she isn't mine. But I work with babies, and I've got this one for the night. I didn't think anyone would mind if I brought her. I mean, I only needed a few minutes to—"

"Are you kidding? Of course it's all right that you brought her." More beaming smiles from Georgia. "So you work with babies, do you?" A fierce look at her three boys. "No one told me that, either. Sit down, sit down."

Phoebe shot him a look then, but what that flash-gash of a look was supposed to mean, he didn't have a clue. A knife suddenly ripped into his side. It had started this morning. Another teensy bomb part, working to the surface, this one above the kidney on the right side. He could see it under the skin. Metallic. Small. In a day or two, it'd wedge to the surface, break through, and then he could try plucking it out like a sliver. But right now, it just plain hurt.

Which ticked him off. He didn't have time for any damn

fool weakness right now. He needed to look normal. He needed to be normal. It was one thing for his family to pester him and another for them to pester Phoebe.

"...baby's name is Christine," Phoebe was saying to his mom. By then she'd been settled in the kitchen rocker and looked like a mythic earth mother, with her arms loosely cuddling the snoozing baby on her stomach. "She was brought to the hospital several days ago. Abandoned, somewhere in the mountains. She'll go into the system—in fact, there's a foster mom already waiting for her. But I've been working with Social Services for a while now on babies like this."

"You mean, baby-sitting them?"

"No, not baby-sitting exactly. More providing a kind of interim care before they're placed in a normal home situation. Abandoned or neglected babies often fail to thrive or fail to bond or both. If they've been hurt that young, they develop an instinctive fear of touch. So I do touch therapy. Love therapy, the social worker calls it—"

"Oh, I love that term," Georgia said delightedly. "What exactly is involved?"

"Different things, really, because every baby's different. But in Christine's case, we're doing what I call a connecting technique. Except for eight hours at night—when I've got an aide to take over—I'll literally keep her attached to me for a solid three days, either directly carried or in the front carrier like this."

"And you do this because?"

"Because we're not sure if she ever learned how to bond. This basically forces the human connection. A real foster or adoptive mom can't do this, of course, but if the ability to bond is there… Mrs. Lockwood, you don't have to go to all this trouble." Phoebe looked stunned at the sweet tea and fresh sugar cookies and apple slices and lasagna being heaped on the table beside her.

"I'm fascinated," Georgia insisted. "In fact, I'd love to hear more. So you—"

Fox cleared his throat. It was nice that the two women were getting along, and that his mom had completely dropped the judgmental kick about Phoebe being a masseuse. But it looked as if the women could talk through the next millennium without coming up for air.

Phoebe immediately looked up at him. There was something…shifty in her eyes. "You're hurting, aren't you?"

Damn woman, kiss her a few times and she thought she knew everything. "No, but—"

"I know, I know. I came to talk about a program for you, and so far all I've done is tie up everyone's time." Phoebe gently rubbed the baby's back as she kept up a soft, steady rocking motion. "The reason I suggested your family listen to these ideas is so they could provide input. You may not go for this at all, Fox. But your family knows more about your health and life issues than I do. And we all need to be on the same team to figure out what motivates you."

Fox frowned. She sounded real sweet, real sincere. Her voice alone aroused every suspicious bone in his body. Something sneaky was coming. Something he didn't want to hear. He just knew it.

Five

Phoebe braced for an explosion. Judging from Fox's thundercloud expression, he definitely hadn't liked the idea that he needed to be motivated—much less that anyone had the power to do it. And if that teensy idea had him already bristling, the rest of her suggestions definitely weren't going to go over well at all.

Phoebe directed smiles at her allies—Bear and Moose and, for sure, Georgia. Fox's mom was adorable. Although her clothes were expensive, she was still wearing a tie-dyed shirt and jeans. And money or no money, she obviously still ruled the roost over her sons, as well.

Phoebe had suffered knots in her stomach when she first walked in here…because, yeah, she'd overhead Mrs. Lockwood's opinion of masseuses. Georgia didn't have a mean bone; she was just expressing the stereotypes Phoebe had heard a zillion times. Masseuses were fine, just not someone you'd want your son to marry. You were happy to go to them for a sore neck, but they made a living touching people, for heaven's sake, so naturally they were on the frayed hem side of respectability.

For two seconds it had hurt Phoebe to hear Fox and his mother talking—but that was foolish. It was one of the main reasons she'd wanted to include his family in Fox's health discussion—so he'd see how a man's mom was likely to treat her.

Christine let out a peep—a little breathy baby snore—and Phoebe rubbed and cuddled her. She'd also brought the baby deliberately. She could have asked her night sub to take over, but truthfully, she figured Fox seeing her with a baby would give him a big, fat, healthy jolt. Babies were a fabulous terror technique for bachelors. Just in case he'd harbored the idea of having wild, uninhibited sex with her, there was nothing like a baby to wilt the *W* right out of that wild. At least for men.

And for herself, she wanted to give up wild, uninhibited sex forever, anyway.

That embrace the other day was still haunting her mind. She simply had to give herself a slap upside the head. It was time to quit mooning over the darn guy and concentrate on her work. She didn't heal well from heartache. Ergo, she needed to stay away from guys who were especially likely to hurt her. Her attraction and pull toward Fox—toward yet another guy who wasn't likely to value or want her long-term—had to be put to bed. Pronto.

And tonight was a terrific chance to make sure he lost interest—assuming he ever had any.

"Okay, now," she addressed his mom and brothers, "these severe headaches Fox gets so regularly…"

"I'm right here," Fox mentioned.

"Uh-huh. They're not exactly migraines or cluster headaches—they couldn't be or I wouldn't be able to dent them with the basic massage techniques I've been using. So we're talking the cause being stress, which one of Fox's doctors already suggested."

"Yeah," Bear and Moose both nodded from across the table.

"I kind of have an unusual view of stress because of my work with babies. In a sense, the babies are suffering from massive stress. They've either been deprived of touch or associate touch with pain—so much so that they've withdrawn from wanting contact. What I do with the babies is a kind of touch therapy to force them—gently—to accept touch. To try to get them to see human contact as something wonderful and helpful."

"I love what you do," Georgia enthused, looking as if she wanted to launch into another round of conversations about babies. Phoebe persevered.

"From everything I've seen…Fox is actually suffering from the same kind of stress. He was hurt. So to protect himself, he's withdrawn. In a way, his headaches function to protect him. So does the rest of his behavior. If he stays in the house, holes up, allows the headaches, he's essentially put himself in a position where he can't be exposed to more pain. You get the concept?"

"Sure," Bear said.

Moose hesitated. "Well, I sure don't. You mean he feels safer if he's hurting? Like those headaches of his are a choice?"

"No. God, no. No one would volunteer for those awful headaches—and all his other injuries are real, besides. But when an animal is hurt, he holes up in his den, right? He rests. He stays away from risk until he's able to handle it again."

"Yeah, I totally get that," Moose said.

"So. Now we have to get Fox out of his den. We have to motivate him to want to get out—which means that we want to supervise his exposure to pleasant and nonrisky experiences."

"Okay, okay, this was cute for a couple of minutes," Fox said irritably. "But enough's enough. I'm not one of your babies. I don't need someone to give me 'pleasant' experiences. I'm not an animal holing up in a den. Phoebe, if you've got some program you want me to do, talk to me, not to them."

Phoebe deliberately tried to make herself sound like a teasing sister. "Now, I can't do that, darlin', because you'd just argue with me. Bear, Moose, I need you on my side if we're going to make this work. You, too, Mrs. Lockwood—"

"Oh, I'm all for whatever you suggest," Georgia said brightly. "This is exactly what Fox needs. To get out of the house, pick up his life again. He's been so depressed."

"I have *not* been depressed," Fox snarled.

The baby stirred again. Phoebe knew the infant would need feeding soon, so she pushed on. "Okay. This is the program. Two times a week I'll do bodywork on Fergus. Some of that'll be massage, concentrating on building strength and stamina. But I also want to teach him de-stress and relaxation techniques—before those headaches get the better of him."

"Sounds like a plan," Moose said.

"Then Moose, Bear...I'm counting on one of you to find the time to take him fishing once a week."

"Fishing?" Bear perked up.

"Fishing? How'd that get into this conversation?" Fergus said disbelievingly, and was ignored.

"I want him out of the house, outside somewhere. I know it's still pretty cold to go out on a boat, but I still like the idea because he couldn't just walk off, go home, you know? He'd have to sit there. And the sun and water could have a real shot at relaxing him."

"You got it. I'm your man," Bear said, and added, "in all the ways you want."

She chuckled at his innuendo. "Thanks, you sweetie. Then, Moose, if you could take him for one evening a week—"

"*Take* me. Like I need a baby-sitter?" Fox snapped.

She honestly didn't want to keep ignoring Fergus, but she still had information to cover, and the baby wasn't going to stay good forever. "Moose, I want Fox doing something stress free, but still something that requires him to get out of the bachelor house. So it'd be a good idea if he went to your place—or any other safe place that would force him out of his rut—"

"I'm sure as hell not in a rut," Fox informed the entire room.

"I was thinking...poker," Phoebe mused. "Something you could do with some guy friends? But if you brothers aren't into cards, I don't care what you choose to do. The point is just getting him out of his den."

"I'm on it," Moose agreed enthusiastically. "Phoebe, I think you're absolutely brilliant."

"I am," she agreed with a chuckle.

"You're not giving me anything to do!" Mrs. Lockwood wailed.

"That's because she's fired," Fox told his mother.

"Now, Fox. You can't fire me because I was never hired. This is just a program plan. Georgia, ideally I'd like you to spend two times a week with Fergus, making him cook."

"Making *him* cook? Instead of me cooking?" The idea was obviously new to Georgia.

"Yes. I want you to have the ingredients and the recipes for his favorite foods around. You do the food shopping so he isn't forced into public quite this fast. But make him do the cooking and preparing, whatever his favorites are. Just supervise. Do it with him."

"What a marvelous idea. Phoebe, it's easy to see why my boys are so in love with you."

Fox raised his hand. "One of your boys is not in love with her. In fact, one of your boys would like to take Phoebe in the backyard for a little personal discussion. No one needs to call the cops or worry if they hear screams. It'll just be me, killing her."

Phoebe refused to laugh, no matter how funny he was being. To his family she said, "I'd like to start this whole program immediately. I know it's late tonight, but I'd still like to take Fox over to my place…give him his first class in pain management." Finally she glanced at Fergus. "Unless you don't need any help with pain control tonight?"

She had him.

She knew she had him.

Something was hurting him. Bad. She knew it from his eyes, from the stiffness in his neck, from his surliness. He wasn't going to turn down help, not when he was this miserable, no matter how much he wanted to.

"I've still got Christine right now...." She patted the pink-blanketed baby again. "But if you'd head over to my place in a half hour or so, Fox, I'll be ready. I was expecting to keep the baby all night, but I have a night sub, Ruby, so it'll take me a few minutes to call her and set that up. After that..." She turned back to his family, not waiting for him to give her any more glares, grief or bologna. "You three can work out your schedules, how and when you can take Fox. But if it's amenable to everybody, I'll take him Thursday and Monday, late afternoon and evenings, all right?"

Bear and Moose heartily agreed, and a few minutes later they walked her out to the van, helping carry her stuff and approving all her ideas with exuberant thumps on the back. They treated her so easily as an honorary sister that Phoebe couldn't help loving them. They were so easy to be with.

So was their mom.

It was just Fergus who made her uneasy.

Just Fergus who itched all her nerves—and hormones, too.

But she'd gained on the problem, she thought tonight. Coming over to his mom's house to discuss the plan for Fergus's recovery had been totally the right thing to do. Meeting his mom, being with his brothers, had helped her get a grip on her emotions, put the whole problem of Fergus in perspective. She needed to stick with a goal she could handle. Helping Fox heal. If she didn't stray off that course, she couldn't possibly get in trouble.

By the time she left she was humming up a storm. Bear

and Moose kissed her cheek goodbye and left her with a chorus of "I love you, darlings" and "Take care of yourself" singing in her ears.

Fox was still scowling when his brothers came back in. He'd seen the guys walk her outside. Seen how their hands were all over her.

"I'm thinking about asking her out," Bear admitted.

"Whoa. I thought you were tight with that teacher in town. Heidi. What's-her-name."

"Yeah, she's nice. But there's no real spark, you know? She's as comfortable as chicken soup. Now, Phoebe, on the other hand—"

"If you don't ask her out, I am," Moose announced.

"Wait a minute." Fox didn't wonder why he was suffering from intense stress—and it had nothing to do with his injuries. Moose was the guy magnet in Gold River, had women climbing all over him—but those relationships never kept his attention more than a few months. Bear was the opposite. Bear was actually looking for a life mate. He'd done the wild oats, done the partying, was starting to look for someone to be with seriously. "Neither one of you is going to ask her out."

"Why?" Both of them asked, and damned if his mother wasn't peering over their shoulders, curious why they couldn't, either.

"Because," he said furiously.

They waited, gaping at him, but he'd said everything he had to say in that single word. And since his side was killing him, he felt completely justified in hightailing it out of there—after thanking his mother for dinner, of course.

He stumbled back to his place and started a shower, hid

under the hot spray, hoping his side would fix—it didn't—hoping the hot water would splash some sense in his head. Which it did. Sort of. He climbed out, pulled on a fresh sweatshirt and jeans and headed out.

He wasn't going to Phoebe's because *she'd* arranged the time, but because he needed to see her. Even if she was using witchcraft or ooga-booga and was a scary, scary woman, the reality still was that no one had fixed his headaches but her. There was nothing wrong with seeking her services.

The problem was that he needed to set up a fair payment schedule for her so they were totally on a business basis. And the other problem was…she bugged him.

In her driveway, Fox slammed the door of his RX 330. Damn woman. How could she possibly know enough about him to get under his skin? When it came down to it, what did she really know about him?

Nothing.

She was bossy. Domineering. Cute. Trouble by any man's definition.

Why did it have to be *her* that made the pain go away? Five million drugs out there, why couldn't one of them work? All the doctors and physical therapists and tests he'd been through and to—none of it had been worth spit. He'd stopped believing anything could help him

He stomped up her gravel drive, scowling at her place. Even in the dimming light, he could see the whole place needed repair. The lawn was a weedfest. A shingle hung crooked from the roof—and if he could see one, there had to be more. And, yeah, he'd seen the inside of her house earlier.

The wild color scheme inside had taken him aback initially…until he'd studied it, figured out what she was doing.

The colors were so striking and interesting that they drew the eye. You noticed the walls instead of what wasn't there, such as furniture. Carpeting. All the stuff that people filled rooms with.

It wasn't Fox's problem if she was living on a financial shoestring, but hell, the whole damn world was greedy today, so why couldn't she be? Instead she was feeding the neighborhood on Saturday mornings. Donating her time weekends, and on nonpaying customers—like him.

That kind of generosity was a disgusting character trait. Who could live with a saint like that?

He barged up to the front door, rapped hard enough to crack his knuckles and then waited. Hissing in air under his breath.

Only…then she opened the door. And there she was, fresh and barefoot, wearing something that looked like pajamas—kind of a pale green, made out of a fabric that made him think of a soft, snuggly rug. Her feet were bare, her hair looped up with some kind of wooden pin holding it together. There was no baby in sight or sound. Somewhere she'd switched a light on, but the light barely trailed as far as the entranceway, creating only enough illumination to make her skin look impossibly soft. Softer than moonshine. Softer than petals. Softer than silver. And then there was the other stuff. She was wearing colors and smells that soothed. Her bare mouth aroused him, so did those sassy-bright blue eyes.

Suddenly it was easy to remember that he was pissed off. He didn't waste time on hello, just went straight for the punch. "This isn't going to work."

She didn't waste time on hello, either. "Yeah it is. Or it can."

He started to walk toward her massage room, but she said swiftly, "Wait, Fox, we're going to the living room."

"Why?"

"Because we're not doing a massage. We're going to do an exercise to help you work with pain. Where is the pain, by the way? It's not a headache this time, is it."

She didn't phrase the comment like a question, which further ticked him off. Damn woman knew things about him that no one could know. "My side's giving me a little trouble. The left side. *Not* something you can help with, and not why I'm here." He aimed his trigger finger at her. "You used my family against me."

"Yup."

"That's unethical. Mean. Underhanded."

"It sure is," she agreed. "Whatever works, huh?"

He wasn't buying into that smile. Not this time. "Don't do it again. If I've got a problem, I solve it. I don't involve family or anyone else."

"Well, of course you don't, you're a grown man. But in this case, your family's pretty frantically worried about you. So now we've given them something to *do.* That may not help you, but it sure helped *them.* Think about it, Fox. I'll bet the bank they'll let up on the heavy-handed caring if they have a constructive way to feel they're helping you."

He thought about that and then scowled. "If you say one more wise thing, I may just put a fist through a wall. There's *nothing* more annoying than a woman who's always right."

"Got it. Heard it before. Let's move along." She motioned to the fluffy rug on the living room floor. "What I want you to do is sit down—any way you want, cross-legged, with a pillow, lying down, whatever's the most comfortable for you."

He sat. Both her pooches beelined for him the instant he

crossed his legs. He'd have scooped them onto his lap if she hadn't crooned, "Mop. Duster. Lie down."

She knelt down across from him—which gave him a binocular shot of the round swell of her breasts, the dip of white skin at her throat. Although her sweater was bulky, it *was* loose at the neck. He wondered if she really believed the cumbersome fabric concealed anything. He also wondered if she ever wore shoes, and how in God's name she'd found a pistachio color to paint her toenails. Her toes were damn near as cute as her—

"Fox," she repeated sternly.

"Pardon? I didn't hear you." He heard the courteous hint of apology in his voice and damned his mother for raising him to be polite to women. "Phoebe, I really didn't come here for any damn fool exercises. I came here to argue about—"

"I understand. You don't like me. You don't want to be here. You're ticked off that I've been able to work with your pain so far, when you'd rather not be asking help from anyone." She said all that smoothly and swiftly, as if to get it out of the way—and as if the damned woman had been reading his mind. "We can fight about all that later, though, can't we? Let's just get this exercise out of the way first. Then you can take all the time you want to rip me up one side and down the other. Take my hands, Fox."

He *knew* she wasn't coming onto him. There was absolutely nothing about her attitude or dress or expression that let on she even remembered the heat of those kisses a few days ago. But for an instant... Fergus mentally corrected himself. It wasn't even an *instant*. Maybe it was a milliinstant. Or a micromilli-instant. But for that micromillisecond of an instant, when she said "take my hands," the image whooshed through his mind of the taste of her mouth.

Of his touching her again.

Of her coming apart for him again.

Of him forgetting the whole damn world with her again.

Naturally that micromillifantasy was absurd and he immediately squelched it…only, it was already too late. The redheaded witch had done it to him again. Forced him to take her hands, forced him to close his eyes, and the next thing she knew, Charlie was stiff as a poker, and Phoebe was forcing him to do ludicrous things.

"Now, Fox…don't talk…don't think. I only want you to do one thing. Imagine. Put a picture in your mind…of the safest place you can possibly imagine. It's a place where nothing can hurt you. Where no one can hurt you. Where you have absolutely no fear of anything."

"Phoebe, I—"

"No. Don't talk. You can in a little bit, but right now—just for a couple minutes—I want you to do this with me. Concentrate. Concentrate with everything you are, on imagining a safe place in your mind." She waited. "Can you invent someplace like that? Imagine it? A place where you know you'd feel completely safe?"

"Yeah."

"Okay. Now keep that picture in your mind and explore it. Look up. Look down. In your mind, pretend you can smell the smells there, hear the sounds there. Know every part of it." She waited. "Are you doing that?"

"Yeah."

"I want you to feel how safe this place is."

"Okay, okay, I feel it." Eyes still closed, he scratched his knee, then stopped, because her voice was flowing over him like music.

"No one can touch you in this place. It's yours and yours alone. No one else has the same safe place you do. No one knows where your place is. And no one can ever take it away from you."

Her voice kept doing that hypnotizing thing—and, yeah, of course he figured out what she was doing. But that didn't seem to be able to stop him from putting this picture in his mind. The picture wasn't anything special. Just a rolling field, a meadow with wildflowers and tall sweet grasses, swaying in a spring wind. Aspens and poplars hemmed the far edge of the field, rustling and shivering in that same breeze. The sun beat down, softer than a balm and healing warm. A bird soared overhead. A fawn cavorted in the grasses. It was a busting-gut happy kind of scene. Nothing hurt. For some crazy, totally insane reason, nothing hurt.

His eyes snapped open. And found Phoebe, still sitting cross-legged across from him, her eyes on his face, her smile on his smile, her scruffy pups snoozing on both sides of her. He said heavily, "This is beyond weird."

"What's weird?"

"Nothing hurts."

"That's great."

"No. You don't understand. I *mean* it. Nothing hurts. Even my *side* doesn't hurt."

"Great."

Before, Fergus thought he'd had enough. But now he'd had *enough*. "This is *not* funny. It's impossible. What'd you do to me?" he demanded suspiciously.

"You did it, not me, Fox. And the exercise won't always

work, but it's always worth a try. So when you feel stress or pain coming on, give it a shot. Go to your safe place."

"That's a pile of hooey," he informed her succinctly.

"Actually, Mr. Skeptic, it's not hooey at all. It's plain old physiology. When you feel pain or stress, your body tenses up. Those tense muscles and tendons essentially cause more pain—whereas when you feel safe, your blood pressure and heart rate both calm down. That helps your body loosen up. Which helps ease the pain. Any exercise that helps you relax would work the same way."

He understood what she was saying. He'd just quit believing in Santa Claus almost three decades ago. Determined to jolt himself back to sanity, he yanked up his sweatshirt on his right side to above his ribs. There, in plain sight, was the needle-size fragment that had been working its way to the surface of his skin for hours now. As Fergus well knew, there was pain and then there was pain. This wasn't bad pain. It was barely mentionable compared to the serious injuries he'd had. But it was what it was—an annoyance. It hurt just enough that he couldn't get it off his mind, the same way it was impossible to ignore a sharp sliver.

Phoebe sucked in her breath when she saw the injury. "What on—"

When he made to poke the spot, she grabbed his hand.

"Are you nuts, Fox? Don't touch that, for Pete's sake! It's an open sore!"

He was speaking to himself more than her. "I *can* still feel it. It's just...*damn*. You were right, Red. Who'd believe it? It's not gone, but it really is nothing compared to how much it was bothering me before."

"That's what I was trying to tell you. That 'safe place' exercise is one way to physically slow down your breathing and pulse. If you can do that, then you're always going to win some over pain. It's not a magic cure. But there are more exercises I can—" She gulped. "Look. Can I take that out? Or do you want to go to a doctor?"

He couldn't twist well enough to see the spot very well—but enough to notice the sliver had broken through the skin. "If you've got tweezers, I can deal with it."

She had tweezers. She had first-aid cream. She had red stuff to wash the spot. She kept him talking while she ran around, accumulating her little tray of supplies, making him explain about the dirty-bomb thing, how parts kept coming to the surface, how that was likely to happen for a while, how it wasn't the end of the world, just disconcerting, and occasionally...gross.

"It's not gross, Fox. That's ridiculous. It's just a sore. But how come no one ever tells us this kind of thing on CNN?"

"Beats me—what are you doing?" He was conscious that for all the touching she'd done to him before, she hadn't actually put her hands below his neck. Not on bare skin. And, yeah, she'd seen him bare that day in the shower, but it wasn't the same thing as having her eyes an inch away from his ribs. Her mouth, her eyes, her face, so close to his heartbeat. So close to his damned ugly scars. "Ouch," he said.

"Darn—did that hurt?" she asked cheerfully, and bent closer with the tweezers again. He could see all that wild, thick red hair of hers, but not her face just then, not the sore. And out of nowhere she suddenly started singing the national anthem.

He forgot the sensitive spot where she was probing. Anyone would. "My God. Is there a cat in heat in here?"

"Fox. This is one long sliver. Are you sure you don't want to go to the emergency room?"

"Hell, no. I can do it myself."

"No, you can't. You can't reach it on your own. It's too far under your arm. Okay, turn a little more this way." When he failed to, she picked up the lyrics. "...what so proudly we hailed..."

He used a cuss word. The big one. And promptly shifted his arm over his head promptly. "I heard you hum before. It was bad, but not this bad. I'll sit as still as you want if you just don't sing again, all right?"

"You promise not to move?"

"I'll promise anything. If you swear you won't sing again."

It was a weak attempt at humor. Very weak. So weak that suddenly neither of them was moving. Somewhere a pup was snoring. Somewhere a faucet was dripping. But the only thing he was really aware of was her face, inches from his. She was looking at him with this...expression. Of caring. And compassion. And something more. Something so gut personal, so intimate, so about her and him, that he couldn't seem to breathe for a whole long second.

And then she said, "It's gone, Fox."

"No, it isn't. It's there every damn time we're in the same room together. Every time you look at me. Every time I look at you."

"No. I mean...it's out."

"I wish I could believe that, but I swear to God, that feeling's coming after us like a freight train. Damn it, Phoebe. I'm not totally sure I planned to have sex again for the rest of my life. I came home not expecting to feel anything for the rest of my life. And then you came along."

"*Fox.* All I'm trying to tell you is that the long metal sliver is out!"

Oh. The sliver. But when he looked at her face again, that fierce, soft look of longing and desire and closeness was still there—real as moonlight. As real as the pulse drumming in her throat. As real as her parted lips.

Six

Phoebe saw him coming, saw him aiming for a kiss, and knew perfectly well he intended trouble—and not a little trouble, but a major-meltdown type of trouble. Yet she couldn't smack him. Not after having seen all those scars, all those healing wounds, all those hurts, so close up. She couldn't do anything to further hurt Fox. It was unthinkable.

Yet when her body bowed toward his—when her lips parted for his—it wasn't exactly because she *wanted* to kiss him. It was just that she recognized his soul needed healing far, far more than his body. And, of course, she had no power to heal his soul or anyone else's. But she couldn't be so mean as to reject Fox.

That was her excuse for kissing him as if she'd die without another taste.

It wasn't because she was a wanton, red-hot mama. It

wasn't because she let her senses rule her sense. It wasn't because she was the kind of woman who'd kick out her morals when a guy turned her on. Phoebe wasn't worried about all those insinuations Alan had implied about her character. She wasn't.

She didn't have time to worry about nonsense like that just then. Her brain was scrambling too hard trying to figure out how to tactfully, carefully, extricate herself from Fox without hurting him. She was fiercely considering that problem. Or trying to—only, by then he was kissing her again. And again. And again.

She fought for a breath. "You're not up for this," she whispered worriedly.

"Oh, trust me. I am."

"I don't want to touch you in the wrong place. Risk hurting you—"

"Phoebe. You couldn't conceivably hurt me in the wrong way. It's the first time I've hurt this good in a lifetime and then some." His hands sieved through her hair. Even in the dusky light, she could see his eyes, fiercer than fire. "Don't stop me. You can stop me later. I swear, I won't go further than you want, not now, not ever. But…don't stop me from kissing you a little more right now, okay?"

If any other man tried that ridiculous line on her, Phoebe would have laughed…but Fox, damn him, wasn't any other man. He sounded as if he really meant it—that he truly believed they'd stop, that he'd stop, that he wasn't just beguiling her into being seduced. And because she believed he was telling her the whole truth—as he knew it—her heart helplessly lunged again.

He'd locked the door on his feelings for so long. It meant

something huge that he'd opened himself now, for her. Yeah, it was sex—she knew it wasn't for more—-but that didn't make his trusting her with his wary emotional state any less. The man was in so much pain. She *had* to respond to him. Anyone would have. Her heart wasn't involved. Not really.

Not exactly.

Oh, hell. Maybe she was falling so deep, so hard in love that her heart was going to get ripped apart and shredded…but right now, holy kamoly, could he kiss.

Since she'd kissed him before, she should have realized how flammable he was. She knew how potent those narrow lips were. How tasty. But he got these terrible inventive ideas this time. His tongue dipped and swirled and teased. His mouth tucked and ducked and tilted and found a hundred new ways to claim hers.

She never took off his sweatshirt, yet somehow it handily dropped to the ground. She swore she never volunteered to touch him, yet somehow her hands were freely running over his chest, his back. She'd touched him before, but she'd touched him as a masseuse.

Now she learned him with a woman's hands, inhaled him the way a woman breathes in her lover. Her fingertips chased over muscles and tendons, over the flat of his stomach, the ridges of ribs, up to the column of his neck—not to chase away knots this time, but to inspire some. Not to ease away sore spots, but to ignore other tactile sensations entirely.

The skin on his shoulder had the vague scent of soap and the naked scent of him beneath that. She caught the hint of musky sweat as he struggled with the heat rising between them, as shocking fast as the gush of a volcano…but that hint of sweat was an aphrodisiac for her. It wasn't work or stress sweat, but simply man sweat, him sweat, the scent of a man on fire.

And still he kissed her. His lips trailed her neck, making necklaces with his damp tongue. His rough, long fingers pushed at her sweater, eased it up and over her head, and on the way back, slowly tugged at her hair. A clip tumbled, then another and another, until her coiled-up hair came apart. So did she.

Mop suddenly clawed at her side. Duster stayed snoring, but Mop tended to worry that her mistress needed rescuing at odd times.

"Lie down, baby," Fox said, in the same tone she used for the dog. Mop obeyed as if she immediately recognized it was okay, it was Fox, not a danger…although he was a danger, Phoebe knew. She'd opened her eyes at the pup's interruption. Now she could see Fox's expression. He stopped moving for that instant, stopped touching her, just took a long, long moment to just look at her.

The last she remembered, they'd both been sitting up, facing each other. Now they both seemed to be lying on the scratchy rug, face-to-face, both of them bare from the waist up. Her yoga pants were tied at the waist, but the ties had loosened and the waistband had dipped below her navel—not revealing anything but the swell of her hip—but he saw that promise of nakedness. He looked. He savored.

He desired.

And so did she. She passionately wanted to be the one who healed Fox. Who made him feel. Who made him *want* to feel again.

She pulled his hand to her breast, encouraged the palm to shape her, to own her. At the same time she pushed at the snap

of his jeans, then chased down the zipper. She'd have lowered the zipper a ton slower if she'd known ahead that the
wicked man wasn't wearing underwear. His jack popped out
of the box so fast it risked being clawed with the zipper
teeth—but she quickly protected him by wrapping her palm
around his long, smooth shift. The flesh was warm and sleek
and pulsed violently inside the circle of her palm.

He hissed in a breath. "Don't."

"Hmm…is that one of those no's that really mean yes?"
she murmured.

"Don't tease."

"You know what, Fox? If there was ever a man who needed
some teasing, I think it's you." As if to prove her point, his
shaft released a single drop of warm, soft moisture. "Oh,
yeah, you like this fine," she whispered, and then suddenly
froze.

In seconds she went from tropic heat to icy Popsicle. The
trigger was hearing her own throaty chuckle, seeing his re-
sponsive lunge to pay her back with the same kind of explo-
sive caresses. Only…she didn't want to be a seducer. Didn't
want him thinking of her as an inhibited easy lover.

The conflict shot anxiety in her pulse with the speed of a
bullet. She wanted him. She totally wanted to make love with
him, to invoke wonderful and healing emotions with him, to
share those feelings together. Only, she didn't want to…give
in, surrender. She could. But she was afraid of feeling
ashamed, the way Alan had made her feel ashamed. She knew
Fox wasn't Alan. Knew it wasn't the same situation at all,
but…

"What's wrong?" Fox whispered between kisses, tracing
the shell of her ear.

She couldn't think when he was touching her. Not like that. Not *really* think. "Fox. You want to make love?"

"You bet the bank I do. With you. Now. If you're willing."

"I am willing. In theory."

"I'm happy with theory," he assured her, as he forged another trail of kisses down her throat.

"But I just don't want you to expect…"

Finally he lifted his head. "Is this that deal from last time? That you don't like sex?"

"I didn't say I didn't like sex. I'm just not a very sexual person, so if you build up a whole bunch of expectations— especially since we barely know each other—"

"Phoebe. You know me better than anyone ever has— whether I want that to be true or not. I may not know you half as well. But how you've gotten through my defenses—my brick walls—tells me this is right. That something is totally right between us. Maybe crazy. But still right." He hesitated. "I can't promise you any kind of future."

"I'm not asking for one."

"It's not you. It's nothing I have against commitment. It's…my life right now."

"I'm not asking for a future," she repeated.

He frowned suddenly, swiftly, as if he were determined to pursue a serious conversation on this. Only, it just wasn't going to happen. Nothing less than a tornado was likely to dim the bright, fierce light in his eyes—the need—not at this moment. "So. You're just not a sexual person," he said in a soft patient tone, as if he were talking a climber down from a perilously tall cliff.

"I'm *not*." At least, she was determined not to be. For him.

"Okay. I'll tell you what. Anything I do that doesn't ring

your chimes, sing out. Will that work?" When she didn't immediately answer—it didn't seem as if he were really expecting an answer—he dove straight for the gold. From those kisses he'd branded on her throat, he worked down, between her cushioned breasts, down into the dip of her navel, then up for the plateau of her white, smooth tummy.

His hands chased down her yoga pants as his tongue and lips continued the same inexorably wicked path. She had no time to tighten up, prepare, brace herself to freeze. She just couldn't make it happen. The breath ached out of her lungs on a lonesome, hungry sigh. Her hands reached for him, needing to touch, to care, to share. To unite.

She tugged the rest of his jeans off as he stole her sanity and inflamed need inside her hotter than a devil fire. She desperately wanted Fox to think she was a good woman. A responsible woman whom he could respect, whom he could count on. He didn't have to love her, but his regard, his respect, mattered more to her than she could even explain.... But this passion between them mattered, too.

She didn't remember ever feeling a burning this hot before. Frustration clawed at her pulse, made her heartbeat go begging. The connection to him...there was just no way to explain, even to her own mind, why she felt so compellingly connected to him....

But it was as if she understood his pain.

It was as if he understood hers.

They rolled off the carpet, back on. Rolled under the soft yellow pool of a lamp's glow, then back in the shadows. It was a good thing she'd been living relatively frugally, because there wasn't much furniture to collide with—still, she would have been more careful with him if he had just let her. For a

man who needed no more bruises, he seemed singularly un-
interested in anything but greedily sipping up every tactile
sensation, every sound, every taste, every cry from her he
could earn or cause.

You'd think the guy had just figured out what was worth
living for.

She had fears. She had seriously sound fears and worries.
But she simply had to give them up. When he loomed over
her, her bare legs wrapped tightly around his waist, she could
no more have denied him than stopped breathing. There was
joy in his eyes. Intense frustration, need sharper than a
knife—but joy, too. That life-shouting zest that only sharing
with another could conceivably inspire....

She took him in. Closed her eyes, lifted her mouth for his,
lifted her hips for his and shimmied until he was seated inside her like in a tight, smooth glove. He let out a growl like
a lion just freed after years in the zoo. She let out a murmur
like a kitten thrilled with her own power.

For an instant they hovered, holding that moment when
he was deep inside her and they were meeting each other's
eyes.

And then they flew. Both rocking to the same rhythm,
beating to the same music, riding the same emotional mountain crest. Sweat gave a sheen to his skin, gilded hers. A
phone rang somewhere. A car backfired. The refrigerator ice
maker clattered a new round of ice cubes.

But not in their world. She held on, eyes squeezed tightly
shut, feeling release pulse through her like a jolt of sweet, hot
electricity. Feeling Fox pulse through her...like a jolt of love
so hot, so sweet, that it sucked her in and under to a whole
new emotional place.

And then she sank back. As he did. Both tried to remember how to breathe normally again.

Minutes ticked by.

She didn't fall asleep, she didn't think, yet it seemed when she opened her eyes, time must have passed, because there was a sweatshirt covering her and Fox was lying on his side, one arm anchoring his head, his other hand drifting through her hair. His eyes had lost that fierce hot intensity and instead simply looked moody dark and fathomless.

"I let the monsters out," he said.

She glanced up, to note both puppies—with wet feet—had taken the best seat in the house while the humans were still on the floor. More moments passed while she absorbed a huge, crazy feeling of total well-being and simple happiness. It felt right, his being with her. Felt perfect, their making love together—like nothing in her life before.

"Hey, you," he murmured, and nuzzled a kiss on her temple.

"Hey, you, back," she whispered.

"Phoebe," he said soberly, "I didn't know that could happen."

"Sex?"

"You're laughing…but yeah. Sex. I really, really didn't know if it would happen for me again in this life."

She sobered, too, then touched his cheek. "What happened to you in the Middle East, Fox?"

"I don't know."

"Yeah, you do."

He hesitated. "I lost me. Lost my belief in myself, my judgment, what I valued about myself. As a man."

"Because of…?"

"It doesn't matter why." Again he brushed a strand of hair from her cheek. "What matters is that I honestly wasn't sure if I'd ever be able to make love again."

She flushed from the toes up, on the inside. From the core of her heart, she'd wanted to help heal him. "I hate to tell you this, big guy, but you gave me signals more than once that your body parts were interested and functioning just fine."

"A hard-on is one thing. Following through is another. And feeling—really feeling—is another." His mind seemed to suddenly change directions, because he went still. "But it's bugging me, Phoebe. That making love wasn't exactly…fair."

She swallowed. "We're having a few regrets, are we?"

"This is the South, red. My mom didn't raise any sons to take advantage of women."

"You didn't take advantage of me."

"Yeah, I did." Mop, as if figuring out the humans were finally, finally returning to real life, scooched over next to his bare hip and resumed the napping position. "I hadn't had sex in a long time. You went totally to my head. That's not an excuse. But it *is* what happened."

"I invited what happened."

"You didn't invite getting involved with a guy whose head is screwed on backward. Who has no life, at least temporarily."

"I knew you were on a recovery track, Fox. Nothing happened that I wasn't allowing to happen."

"That wouldn't count worth beans with my mama, let me tell you." He was joking, doing the Southern gentleman thing. But he'd stopped playing with her hair, stopped touching her. Stopped staying in touch with her. "You've got a right to more than I offered you, Red…but it's not that easy for me to come through. At least not yet. I need to think—a ton—before even trying to talk more about this. For tonight…I'm going home."

"Yes. I assumed you would." She didn't freeze inside. She'd never—once—assumed that he'd stay after making love with her. It was just sex they'd had. It wasn't a relationship. It was what it was, and there was no hurt spiking its way into her heart.

"For the record, though…I'm going to try your recovery program."

"Good. I think it's worth trying. It's all stuff that's good for you."

"It may be. You haven't had a wrong idea about my state of health yet—even if you've been aggravating the hell out of me."

"You're awfully easy to aggravate, Fox."

"Then how come other people can't seem to do it? I know you won't believe this, but everyone who knows me thinks I'm the most patient guy this side of the Atlantic."

"You've fooled all of them?" she said with surprise, and made him grin. But not for long.

"I'll do your program. But this is the deal. First, I'm going to pay you by the hour." He mentioned a sum.

"I don't need to be rolling in diamonds, slugger. This is what I charge—"

"I don't care what you charge. That's what I'm paying you. And another thing—"

"What?"

He motioned to the far archway, where the hall led down to the business part of house. "I'll build your waterfall."

"I don't think you're up for that kind of heavy work—"

"If I can't, I can't. But I'll try. When my dad died, he left my mom financially secure enough, but she was still determined that we'd all know how to do things, not be dependent on others. So I know some plumbing and carpentry. Depending on how my body holds out, I can do the work. And that'll be part of my payment to you. Money. But the waterfall, too."

When he left, she found herself standing naked in the dark window, watching the lights of his vehicle pull out and then disappear into the night. All that extraordinary postsex euphoria and closeness seemed to vanish faster than a light switched off…and a sick feeling of fear replaced it.

Mop moaned next to her ankles, until Phoebe picked up the disgraceful whiner and cuddled him under her chin. Still, she stared out the dark window, thinking fiercely that she felt good about making love with Fox. She *did*. Totally good. Really. It was just…

Vague memories zipped through Phoebe's mind, of her childhood. Her mother had been a hard-core earth mom and emotional hedonist. Her dad had adored those qualities in her and valued her in every way. It was so easy to grow up believing that sensuality was healthy and a wonderful part of being a woman. Her dad called her pure female, and meant it as the warmest of compliments.

And every media source in the universe taught a girl that men wanted a sensual woman. A hot, willing, uninhibited woman who freely expressed her sexuality was the ideal, right? Every man's dream, right?

Wrong.

At her feet, Duster suddenly yipped, clearly miffed that Mop was being held and she was being ignored, so Phoebe had to scoop her up and cuddle her, too…but that sick, wary feeling inside kept turning in her stomach. Men wanted a "hot" woman, all right. But only to sleep with, not to keep. Something in a man distrusted a woman who was too open with her sexuality. They feared she wouldn't be faithful. Feared they couldn't trust her. Something deep inside just didn't respect a woman like that.

Phoebe had learned it all the hard way from Alan. The part that really bit was his accusing her of being a hedonist and sensualist—because she couldn't defend those charges. She very definitely was those things. He'd made her feel so dirty that she'd started to think of herself the same way...until she switched her career from PT to massage work with babies.

She hadn't thought of Alan in months...until Fox entered her life. She knew the men were completely unalike. But she still feared ever falling for someone again who didn't, or couldn't, completely respect her.

Abruptly she turned around and aimed for the back door so she could let the pups out one last time before bed. The cool draft of air on her bare skin made her shiver, helped her face more reality.

She refused to regret making love with him. Helping Fox regain his life really mattered to her—no matter what she had to do, no matter what the emotional cost to herself. She just had to remember how this night had ended.

He hadn't wanted to stay all night with her after making love.

And he'd pretty damn violently been insistent on paying her—hugely—for her services.

She got it. If she could heal his wounded soul, she wanted to. She just couldn't kid herself that he valued her as more than the hired help. For a few hours, there, she'd felt such an extraordinary connection to him…. She'd felt like a soft, fragile rose, petals opening inside her that had been sealed shut for so long…but she knew better. Really.

To Fox she was a masseuse. As long as she guarded her heart from wanting to be more in his life, there was no problem.

And she wasn't about to forget that again.

Seven

In a single week, nature had blown off winter and poured in spring. Bright-yellow azaleas bloomed everywhere. The sun shone through sassy-green fresh leaves. Sleepy, sneaky breezes teased the senses.

The earth and grass smelled pungent, as if every spore and root under the surface was having sex and about to burst into life.

Except for him, Fox thought glumly.

Just because he'd had heart-destroying sex with Phoebe once, of course, was no reason to assume they'd have it again. There were compelling reasons why they shouldn't, besides. Only...

Only, he wanted to have sex with her.

Immediately. Regularly. Preferably on the hour. For several weeks nonstop.

Right or wrong had nothing to do with it. His hormones only understood that issues of values were inconsequential. Having had her, he wanted more. He wanted. Her. No one else. Nothing else. And his hormones kept beating that same drum, day after day after day.

"What in God's name are you doing?" Bear asked dryly.

Fox glanced up. It was a Bear day—which meant, according to Phoebe's ridiculous recovery program—that he was supposed to be fishing. For the cause—and fishing was always Bear's favorite cause—he'd dragged him across the border into South Carolina. Any other time, Fox wouldn't have minded. Lake Jocassee was a serious piece of paradise—one of those God's-country kinds of places. The reservoir of cold, clear water was back-dropped by sunlit knolls and mountains, mostly undeveloped—and everyone loved it that way.

Bear had trailered the boat, bought the live bait as well as a box of proven lucky lures, stashed Fox in the bow and puttered off for an ideal fishing spot. Jocassee was known for trophy trout—also for bass, but it was the brown and rainbow trout Bear wanted for dinner. At this time of day and year fishing wasn't ideal, but that didn't deter Bear, who'd already hooked enough to bring Mom two dinners, easy.

Now, though, Bear had unfortunately been distracted. "What are you *doing*?" he repeated.

"What do you mean, what am I doing? I'm sitting here with you."

Bear sighed and then leaned over to grab one of the books from Fox's lap. He started reading the titles aloud. *"Women and the Law of Property in Early America. The Politics of Social and Sexual Control in the Old South."* Bear scowled at him. "You call this kind of reading relaxing?"

"Well…yes, actually."

"And you think you're convincing anybody you'll never be a history teacher again?" His brother's voice dripped humor.

"This has nothing to do with teaching! This is pleasure reading!"

"Yeah, right. The point, anyway, is that you're supposed to kick back and *fish*. Phoebe told you—"

"All Phoebe insisted on was that I get out of the house. So I'm in the incessant fresh air. What she wanted. That doesn't mean I have to like fishing."

"It isn't human to hate fishing."

"How long are you going to hold that against me? Give me a ball—foot, base, basket, soccer, whatever, and I'll whip the pants off you in any of those sports. But sitting here torturing worms on hooks…" Fox shook his head.

"I'll tell Phoebe on you if you don't at least pick up a pole."

"That," Fox said darkly, "is an ugly, ugly threat. Did I tattle on you when you and Moose put the skunk in the school cafeteria? Did I tell Moose when you threw up on his favorite shirt in high school? Brothers never tell."

"That was completely different. This is for your own good. Reading a bunch of history is not *relaxing*. Not the way Phoebe said we were supposed to make you. You're supposed to have *fun*."

"Reading *is* fun," Fox said firmly, and opened a book again. He didn't know which book, because he'd given up trying to concentrate a good hour before. The sun poured on his head, his shoulders. The lake was so clear he could see several mesmerizing feet below. Normally the lake—or reading books he loved—really would have relaxed him. It was just that right now, the only thoughts in his head were about Phoebe.

So maybe they'd only made love once. And possibly it had been ten days, twelve hours and seven minutes since that once, but the entire encounter was still diamond clear in Fox's mind—and not just the naked parts either.

One of the things that bugged him was how—twice now—she'd suddenly upped and claimed that she didn't have a sexual nature. Both times she'd been in the middle of kissing him senseless. It'd be funny if it wasn't so…odd. Since she was obviously a natural sensualist to the core, Fox couldn't fathom why she'd claim something so ridiculous—or want him to believe it.

Of course, all women were impossible to understand at a certain level, so Fox wasn't dwelling on just that one thing. Other details about that night still tantalized and frustrated him, as well. Color was one. She had all those colorful rooms in her house—blue, green, yellow and all—yet he still hadn't seen her bedroom or what color she'd painted it. And then there was the critical issue of panties.

She'd been wearing yoga pants that night. It was typical of her to wear comfortable, easy-moving clothes, but underneath those figure-concealing pants he recalled—in total and exquisite detail—her panties. They'd been thongs. Satiny. They'd been white except for the heart-shaped spanking-red bitsy front patch—which, actually, a guy nearly needed magnifying glasses to see at all.

Still, Fox happened to have been that close up. He *had* seen. And they seemed like a fairly astounding choice of panties for a woman who tended to wear oversize sweaters and pants. Same issue with the house. She'd painted all those sensual, soft colors—yet she freaked if you mentioned that she had a sensual side.

Something was wrong, Fox thought. Well, hell. A lot was wrong, as far as his coming on to a woman when he couldn't offer her a damn thing. But besides that…something was wrong with Phoebe. Wrong *for* Phoebe. She was a life lover, a giver, a hedonist, a dare anything kind of woman who stood up. She understood his heart and his feelings better than he had.

She'd helped him so much with her generous, giving ways that it bugged him all the more that there was this problem. This *something* in her that was off. It was as if she were afraid, or wary. But of what?

"And the other thing that bothered me was her saying she didn't care if there was a future," he said irritably.

"Huh?"

"For Pete's sake, what kind of attitude is that? I mean, it's one thing if people can't work out a relationship—not that I like the *r* word. It's a stupid word. But when it comes down to it, you meet someone, you work at it, and then it either works out or it doesn't, right?"

"I think you're getting dehydrated. There's more ice water in the thermos," Bear said patiently.

"I'm just saying, when things go wrong, it doesn't have to be about *blame*. Usually both people try. Nobody goes into a deal thinking they're going to deliberately hurt the other person. I mean, unless they're complete dolts."

"Okay. Beats me who you're talking to, but I'm for the conversation. If we're going to talk about women, though, I think we should talk about Phoebe."

Fox suddenly jerked his head around and focused on his brother. "What? I wasn't talking about Phoebe."

"I didn't say you were," his handsome older brother said cheerfully, but then didn't speak further because there was a tug on his line. The whole world stopped for a trout. Who could figure. This one was a rainbow, maybe nine inches, fought like a boxer—and won. "Hell," Bear said, when the fish freed itself from the line and took off.

Finally. "What were you going to say about Phoebe?" Fox demanded.

"Well…a couple weeks ago when her name first came up, I was just teasing about asking her out. But April and I quit even playing at making something happen between us. Not like we had a big thing going, anyway. The point, though, is that I really am thinking about asking Phoebe out now."

"No."

"No why?"

"No because."

Bland-faced, Bear tried laying out a few of his dating credentials. "I make good money. Great money, in fact. Got good family genes, can offer a woman security, and I figure I'm pretty close to wanting to settle down. It's been years since I had fun waking up with a hangover and a new woman. Just no interest in catting around anymore. I'd like a couple of rug rats. A woman I could talk to, be with every night—"

"And that's fine, just fine. You're getting really old," Fox assured him. "You need to settle down. But not with Phoebe."

"Ah. I get it now."

"You get *what* now?"

"Moose knows it, too," Bear said smugly. "That you've got a thing for her. We just weren't sure how serious it was."

"I don't—can't—have a thing for anyone. You think I'd

ask a woman out when I don't even have a job? Don't have a clue what I'll be doing even next month?"

"Okay, so right this exact minute you're not on track yet," Bear agreed. "But you only had two of those hellion headaches last week."

And one, Fox thought, that he'd actually dented with that ridiculous exercise of hers—not that he could admit that in public. Even to a brother.

"What I was trying to say," Bear went on, "is that you finally seem to be headed uphill, Fox. You're not completely well yet, but you're definitely on an uphill road. So…"

"So?"

"So, I'll tell you what. I may or may not ask Phoebe out. But I'll wait until you've finished the whole month's program that she created, okay? Until you're better. And that really is the key."

"*What* key?" Sometimes following Bear's conversations was like interpreting politics. You had to weed through the words to get to the meaning. Assuming there was one.

"The key," Bear said patiently, "is that you need to get better. It's the best offense and defense you have. That woman's got you tied up in knots. When you get better, you'll be strong enough to untie the knots, to figure what you really want out of the situation."

Fox opened his mouth, closed it. He wanted to argue furiously that neither Phoebe nor any other woman had him tied up in knots or ever would, but there wouldn't be much point in that. She did. Period.

But that didn't mean Bear had everything right. Fox loved his brother, but Bear was almost always wrong, and this was no exception. He couldn't possibly wait until he was stronger to fix the situation with Phoebe. Truth was, he doubted he could stand waiting even another minute.

A guy couldn't just make love with a woman—not when the emotional connection had rocked his world inside and out. And then just go back to do those pansy "safe place" pain exercises as if he and Phoebe were nothing more than accidental business acquaintances.

He couldn't let her get away with it. Healing him and loving him and giving 300 percent to him at every turn—and then taking zippo in return. The more Fox dwelled on it, the more he realized that he simply had to find out what was bugging her. Either that or risk losing what little mind he had left, because for damn sure, he couldn't think of anything *but* her until they got this settled.

And after they got this all settled, then they'd make love again.

The more Fox thought about it, the more he figured he had a good plan coming together.

He was still feeling confident the next day, when he parked in her driveway and stepped out, carrying an impressive array of tools. The tools weren't totally a disguise. She did, after all, have a waterfall that needed constructing. But as he lifted a fist to rap on her front door, he heard the unexpected sound of crying from somewhere in the house. A baby's crying. And not a little mournful wail, but a full-scale, nonstop scream, as if someone were torturing an infant.

No one could be torturing an infant at Phoebe's place— not if she were alive—so naturally he panicked. Either there'd been an accident or some other crisis must have happened. So he pushed open the door, yelled out that he was here, and charged toward the sound of the crying.

He found Phoebe almost immediately, standing in the kitchen, stuffing some kind of long-stemmed, sweet-smelling, sissy purple flowers in a vase. She was barefoot—no surprise. Wearing a long jeans skirt, and a loose tee in bright red. Something bubbled in a pot on the stove—something with garlic and rosemary and some other unidentifiable saucy smell. It was the kind of mysterious sauce smell that could bring a man to his knees. Easily. Phoebe's back was to him. She was humming softly, moving to an R&B tune played low on the radio as she fixed her flowers and occasionally stirred the pot. The whole scene looked wonderful…except for the shrieking infant in the front pack strapped to her tummy.

She spun around when she sensed him in the doorway. "Well, hey you." Her smile was bright and sexy…but not particularly personal. "Did I goof up the schedule? It's just Wednesday, isn't it? You're not due until tomorrow, are you?"

The cheerful question slugged him straight in the gut. It was her reference to "the schedule." How easily, this whole last week, she'd treated him as a client instead of a lover. He scraped a hand through his hair. "No, but I—"

"It's okay," she said in a normal voice, as if anyone could hear over the infant's caterwauling. "Come on in. You're welcome to visit. It's just that I have Manuel…and the odds of Manuel being quiet are about a thousand to one."

She didn't look shaken by the baby's screams. As busy as she looked, her left hand stayed in touch with the little one, rubbing and loving and consoling. Because of the baby's name, Fox assumed it was a boy; otherwise it would have been impossible to tell. The head was bald, the face all squinched up and red from the screaming.

"Manuel came from Chicago," Phoebe filled in.

"How come you got a baby from so far away?"

"I don't, usually…but I've had contacts with different agencies across the country for a while now. Everybody's got the same problems. What to do with throwaway babies. How to turn a baby around when there's been no bonding or care to start with." She ambled over, carrying a wooden spoon, lifting it for him to taste. "More salt?"

He tasted. "It's perfect."

"I dunno. I think it still needs something. Maybe a little more garlic or more tarragon…anyway. The crime statistics alone could put hair on your chest. Look at a kid in trouble, you'll almost always find a baby who didn't bond, didn't get the nurturing he needed. I don't have this little sweetie for long. Just three days."

"Three days is enough to matter?"

"Yes and no. Yes, loving time—touch time—with a baby always matters. And it'll hopefully be enough to see if we can start him on a different road…"

Fox was interested in the details. The work she did fascinated him. But just then it was hard to concentrate. "You're sure he's not sick?"

"Positive."

"You're sure he's not hungry or dying or anything? I mean, the way he's crying—"

She nodded. "It sounds inhuman, I know," she said softly. "His birth mom was an addict, so this little darling came into the world in agony. He's been through the whole withdrawal procedure, so at this point he isn't feeling the craving for drugs so much as…anger. Misery at being alive. And maybe we can't help him, but you know, we can't just keep throwing babies away—"

No, he didn't know. He also didn't know how Phoebe could think, much less calmly hold a conversation, with a baby crying that relentlessly. But for damn sure, the part of his plan about talking with her—and then making love—fizzled fast.

It was a shocking moment to realize he'd fallen hopelessly in love with her. Not just because the chances of their making love any time in the immediate future were completely annihilated. But she was standing there in her bare feet, with the screaming baby and the spoon, backed by all her candy-colored rooms…and there it was. This overwhelming emotion, when he could have sworn he was no longer capable of any feelings, much less real ones. Yet just looking at her sucked him in so deep, so rich, that he could have died and gone to heaven, thrilled just to be with her in the same damn room for that instant in time.

"You came over for a reason this morning?" she asked, just as if they'd been having a normal conversation.

"Yeah—I didn't know if you were going to need the therapy room, but if it was free during the lunch hour, I figured I'd get some work done on the waterfall."

"Oh! That's great. And the room's free—Manuel is all I'm trying to do today. I do have to wander back there now and then—"

"Well, will it bother him if I'm making noise?"

"Everything bothers him," she said, with a tender pat on the baby's diapered rump. "But it doesn't matter. It's the best thing for him to be exposed to normal sounds, normal life—because that way he finds out he'll be protected no matter what's happening around him. So go for it."

He went for it.

First off, he hunkered down in the corner of her massage room and studied all the supplies she'd bought and her master plan. Good thing he had a contractor for a brother who could railroad the applicable licenses—and double good thing that his mom hadn't raised any sons who ducked hard work. Act One had to be the plumbing, and after that he could move on to the easy stuff—mortar and stone and tiling. Big messes. Big weight. Big work—at least for a guy who could barely bend without creaking and groaning. It was going to take some mighty long hours to build this insane indoor waterfall she wanted.

But it was so like her—to value something sensual and beautiful over something practical. And it was a way to do something for her. A way to give back. As far as Fox could tell, too damn many people took from Phoebe without her letting on that she needed anything—much less took anything—from anyone.

He poured on the coals, knowing that his body would give out quickly from this kind of physical work. He didn't realize how he'd become used to the sound of the baby crying, until there was suddenly silence. Instinctively he leaped to his feet, thinking that damn squirt must have died, and raced back through the house so panicked he forgot about his dusty hands and safety goggles.

He found Phoebe in her odd little mint-green room—the closet turned into an office. She was sitting at a desk, paying bills, the baby sleeping on her tummy.

Actually sleeping. He checked by hunching down and looking.

"It won't last," Phoebe whispered humorously. "But, yeah, he really is napping."

"Any chance he'll do this for a while?" Hell. He was afraid to even whisper.

"I dunno. When a baby's born addicted, one of their problems is that they can't rest. This little one's past that…but he just seems angry all the time. No one got around to giving him a reason for living, you know?"

Fox said soberly, "Yeah. I do know."

Phoebe glanced at him with suddenly sharp eyes. She opened her mouth—he knew she was going to start asking questions—so he swiveled around quickly and headed back to work.

A half hour later he heard the baby start wailing again—followed by Phoebe's slow, ever-patient, soothing voice and her ghastly off-key humming. A few minutes after that she showed up in the doorway.

"Are we going to be in your way if I give him a bath here, Fox?"

"No sweat." He was nowhere ready for power-tool noise yet. He was still interpreting the plumbing instructions, laying out the fittings. And he kept at it, although he watched her from the corner of his eye and became more and more confused at what she was doing. She filled up the big claw-footed bathtub in the middle of the room. The location of the tub didn't surprise him; he'd just figured she used it for physical therapy, but it was huge, hardly baby-size. He'd have thought the sink would be a lot easier way to bathe a baby that little. But he'd stopped talking by then, didn't want to interfere, and truth to tell, he'd sunk into a skunky mood. Her comment had done it, the one about how the baby hadn't found a reason for living.

His mind kept jolting back to the little dark-haired boy—

the one in his nightmare, the one he'd tried to approach. The one he'd tried to show that there were people in this life who could be trusted, who wanted to help, who'd reach out. Everyone in his family and circle of friends had fought him about going into the military. They said it was a crazy choice for a man who hated guns, but they didn't get it. That was the point. That he hated guns. That he loved children. If people didn't stand up for kids, didn't take a risk and reach out, how was anything going to change?

Aw, hell. Whenever his mind crept down those dark alleys, he always seemed to sink like a stone. He could feel the ugliness creeping inside him, the darkness he'd been trying to swim out of for weeks now. Or at least he'd been trying to—since Phoebe.

And there she was, suddenly. When the tub was full, she stripped the baby of clothes and diaper—no surprise—but the surprise when she scooped the baby into her arms again and stepped into the tub.

His jaw dropped.

She wasn't naked herself. She had on a little T-shirt and boxers. But he'd just never expected her to climb in the bath with the baby. The little one almost immediately stopped crying—possibly from shock, possibly because it liked the warm water. Who could guess?

But she laughed with delight, praising him softly, gently. "So is water going to be your Achilles' heel, Manuel? Because if we've finally found out what turns you on, little one, we're going to be wet a lot…."

Finally he understood what she was doing. She'd already told him that her intent was to stay physically in touch with the baby 24/7 if possible; he just hadn't realized that meant *really* 24/7—that even in activities like a bath, the baby would have her to hold on to, like now. Naked as a newborn, he was lying on her tummy, feeling her security, her hands, the warmth of her heartbeat.

Fox's pulse suddenly drummed, drummed. She was really a damned extraordinary woman. Her confidence with the baby, her endless patience, the love she gave so freely, so generously…God. It was no wonder he couldn't help loving her. What human being could *not* love her?

But it still ripped through his mind that there'd been a time he'd had confidence and patience. A time he'd believed he even had a gift with kids. Kids had always been his calling. He'd really believed it.

But that sure as hell wasn't true anymore.

"Fox?"

He turned around at the doorway, carrying his jacket and tool box. "I didn't want to interrupt the two of you. But I have to go."

"Right this second? You weren't going to say anything?"

"When the kid wasn't crying?" He motioned toward the work corner. "I know I left it a complete mess, but I'll be back later. I figured I'd just cover it up for now." Both theoretically and symbolically, he thought.

"You're due over tomorrow night for your session."

"Yeah, I know." But right then he felt the worst hell-hot headache coming on that he'd suffered in a while. He knew it was bad. The kind that would make him sick as a dog. He just wanted to get out of there and get home.

And right then he was unsure whether he was coming back. Ever.

Eight

Phoebe lit the melon-scented candle and blew out the match. She stepped back with her hands on her hips and surveyed the table worriedly. Mop and Duster both yipped, just in case she'd forgotten they were there. They certainly couldn't forget the fabulous smells drifting from the stovetop, and for some God unknown reason, no one was giving them tidbits.

Phoebe had given the beggars plenty of treats, but right now she was too concerned about Fergus to concentrate on anything else.

The rap on the front door inspired the dogs to race, barking the whole time, to great the visitor. Phoebe had barely opened the door before they leaped on Fergus, but when he looked up from the petting frenzy, his eyes were definitely only on her.

"I *am* due here tonight, right?"

"Right." She *knew* how he could make her feel, yet still had to fight the rush and her zooming pulse rate. Naturally he was surprised to find her dressed differently, because he never saw her in anything but loose-fitting clothes. Form-fitting attire would hardly work for a masseuse. Her soft black sweater and slacks were hardly sexy—she didn't do sexy—but yeah, she'd made a different kind of effort tonight. She still hadn't put on shoes because she never wore shoes if she could help it, but she'd brushed her hair loose and put on a little face goop. Not much. Just some lip gloss, a little blush, a little mascara.

Judging from the dangerous glint in Fox's eyes, you'd think she'd put on major war paint.

She led him toward the kitchen, musing that she *had* strategized a major war effort tonight. From her clothes to the setting, she'd wanted to create something that would startle him—because she had really, really doubted he intended to show up today.

Something had been seriously wrong when he left two days ago. She didn't know what, but in the space of a short conversation, Fergus had changed from a recovering, functioning, whole-hearted guy back into a taciturn shadow again. When he'd left, she'd desperately wanted to chase after him and confront whatever was wrong—but she'd had the baby to take care of. Besides which, she'd realized joltingly that she had no right to chase after him—that she had no personal right to care about Fergus.

Tonight, though, she'd convinced herself that her strategic choices were all strictly professional. His recovery was her business, right? So if she chose to wear a snuggly black sweater and if it happened to catch his attention—as long as it was for a professional reason, that was okay.

He asked about Manuel, and they chatted a few minutes about the baby and how her work was going. Since he was only planning to stay for the usual two-hour session, though, she needed to hustle the dinner along, and motioned him to sit down. "I have another exercise for you to try today."

"Oh, yeah?" He didn't seem to notice the candles, the linen, the setting she'd worked so hard on. The darn man hadn't taken his eyes off her yet. It was downright distracting. "What are those smells?"

"Dinner."

"Dinner wasn't part of the deal," he said.

"It is today. Anything's part of the deal that puts you on a healing track, cookie."

"Cookie?" He almost choked on the teasing endearment, but she just chuckled—and put on oven gloves. Her scarred relic of a kitchen table had been covered with an elegant navy blue tablecloth—alias a bed sheet. She'd dimmed the lights, set up a centerpiece of melon-, peach- and strawberry-scented candles. Scraps of navy velvet ribbon tied the silverware, since she didn't own real napkin holders.

The menu was far from gourmet. Hot buttered, homemade bread. The potato dish everybody made for holidays with sour cream and corn flakes and cheddar cheese. Chicken rubbed with fresh cilantro and island pepper. Fresh cherries and blueberries, and eventually, a marshmallow sundae with double-chocolate ice cream. All easy, basic stuff. All comfort food.

Fox, though, raised an eyebrow as more bowls and plates showed up on the table. "What is this?"

"Like I said—just dinner."

"This is 'just dinner' like a diamond is 'just a stone.' You think I can't tell when a woman's determined to seduce me?"

"What?" She dropped a hot pad. Then a fork.

"Give me a break. You know what the smell of homemade bread does to a guy's hormones, don't you?"

He was teasing with her. Flirting. Her heart soared a few thousand feet—not because he made her feel mooshy inside, but because, darn it, all the risks she'd taken for him really were paying off. For him, if not for her. Even a few weeks ago, he'd still been locking himself in a dark room, unwilling to be around people and, for darn sure, stingy with his smiles.

"The homemade bread was about motivating your hunger," she insisted.

"That's exactly what I said. That the smell of homemade bread is a foolproof way to motivate hunger in a guy. Better than just about anything on earth—give or take that sweater you're wearing."

"It's just a sweater, Fox! I—" The cell phone chimed, forcing her to peel off an oven glove to answer it.

It was her mom, and because it was an unusual time for her mother to call, she motioned to Fox that she'd just be a few seconds, and continued bringing on the food. "There's nothing wrong is there, Mom? You're okay? Dad's okay?"

"Everything's fine." Her mother's magnolia-sweet voice was a little too careful, but Phoebe swiftly learned why. "I just wanted to tell you something, honey. I saw in the paper tonight that Alan's getting married. I know you two are long over, but I just didn't want any stranger springing the news on you...."

The chicken was going to dry out if she didn't get the dinner served, so she promised to call her mom later and hung up as quickly as she could, then hustled to sit across from Fox.

"Sorry about the interruption," she said with a smile. "I talk to my mom a few times a week, but we still never seem to be able to have a short conversation."

"She said something that bothered you?"

"Oh, no. Everything's fine."

"She must have said something or told you something—"

To ward off another direct question, Phoebe served potatoes—no man alive so far had ever resisted those potatoes—and freely offered him some of her family background. "My dad and mom are both from Asheville. Dad's an anesthesiologist. My mom always claimed it was a good thing he made good money, because she was too lazy to work—but that was a complete fib. She's a hard-core volunteerer. Works with sick kids at the hospital. And troubled teenagers at a runaway place. And she's on the board of directors for an adoption agency. She never stops running…. She also paints."

"So that's where all these colors come from?" He motioned around her house.

"Oh, yeah. Mom definitely taught me not to be afraid of color."

"You sound pretty close."

"Couldn't be closer. Same for my dad."

"So what'd she say that bugged you?"

Her smile dipped, but only for a second. "Fox," she said firmly, "this is about you. Your time, your dollar. I don't mind talking about myself, but not when we're working together." She glanced at his plate, though, and realized he was on his second helping. "Forget it. Ask me anything you want."

"Pardon?"

She motioned. "Look at you. Eating like a pig. I'm so

proud." She passed him the plate of warm bread again. "Okay, I forgot, what was it you wanted to know?"

"What your mother said. And I'm *not* eating like a pig."

"Come on, you," she crooned. "Try the glazed carrots. The recipe's so good you won't even realize it's a vegetable, I promise. She was just telling me that a man I used to know was getting married."

"I take it you and this guy were a thing?"

"Yup. Was engaged to him myself, in fact. She was afraid I'd be shook up and hurt when I found out about it."

"So…are you? All shook up and hurt?"

"Do I look remotely shook up?" But over the flickering candlelight, she saw his expression. "Damn. Quit looking at me like that, Fox. Go back to eating."

"How long were you with the guy?"

"Three years. Close to four."

"So he's the one you broke up with. The reason you moved here."

"Yes, Mr. Nosy. If you want the down and ugly, he broke my heart. Bad enough that I couldn't seem to shake it without moving to a new place, totally starting over, physically and emotionally. But that's water way over the dam now. Eat those carrots."

He was. But he was still like a hound with a bone. "How did the son of a bitch break your heart?"

She waved the royal finger at him. "Normally I wouldn't care what language you use. I can do all the four-letter words myself. But not tonight, Fergus. The whole dinner and program tonight is to coax you to feeling calm and relaxed. To help you heal. That's not going to happen if you get yourself all revved up."

"I'm not revved up. I just want to know what the bastard did. Cheat on you?"

"No."

Fox suddenly slammed down his glass of water. "Hell. He didn't hit you, did he?"

She raised an eyebrow. "Did you forget who you were talking to? No one in this life is going to hit me and live to tell it."

He nodded. "Yeah, that was a foolish fear, Red. Zipped out of my mouth before I stopped to think. Any guy who'd try that kind of nonsense wouldn't still be alive. And you sure wouldn't have mourned him."

"You've got that right."

Fergus heaped another helping of potatoes on her plate. "You're tough and strong and can take care of yourself. No question about that. So what exactly did this guy do to hurt you?"

She sighed. "I'll answer that. I'll even give you the long, boring, embarrassing answer—but you'll have to answer something for me first. I want to know what happened. In the Middle East. I know the cover story, how you were hit with a dirty bomb and all. But I want the details. Where were you, what was going on, what was the whole shemola."

It was his turn to hesitate. In fact, he apparently wanted to avoid that question so much he scooped up their empty plates and carted them to the sink, then turned around to give her one of those fierce, glowering looks that always successfully made his two big brothers back off pronto.

It didn't work on her. She just had a feeling this was it— it with a capital *I*. Either they had some kind of breakthrough together or he was going to back off from seeing her—not because she hadn't helped him with the pain, but because something in Fox wasn't sure he wanted to heal.

Surprisingly he ambled into an answer, as if the subject bored him but he was willing to go along with her. At least for a while. "I enlisted in the service because of the kids. Because teachers need to be role models for kids, and history teachers get stuck being role models of a unique kind. Every day, see, I was talking about heroes in American history. What made a hero. Why we studied certain men and women over others. How we defined leadership and courage and all that big hairy stuff."

"Okay." Since he was clearing away the dishes, she stood up, too. The dogs trailed her like hopeful shadows. She slid them scraps, washed her hands, then brought out her ruby-glass bowls and the double-chocolate ice cream. Then waited.

"Okay," he echoed her. "So a part of teaching history is teaching heroes—teaching kids that all of them had the potential to be heroic in the right circumstance. That being a hero wasn't about having courage. It was about finding courage. That everybody was vulnerable and scared sometimes, but that the right thing to do is to stand up for people more vulnerable than you are."

God. He was going to turn her into mush. She heaped five big globs of ice cream without even thinking. Her heart just squished for what he said, how he said it, what he so clearly believed from his heart. But she said just "okay" again as if leading him to continue.

"So…" He fed plates into the dishwasher as if he were dealing cards, whisk, whisk, whisk. "So there came a point when we came to a unit about the Middle East, talking about history there, what had been happening over the last several decades specifically. The problem, as I could see it, was that the grown-ups in their families tend to wring their hands about anything to do with Middle East, you know? Everybody's tired of trying to fix something that nobody thinks we can fix. Of trying to do something we don't have the power to do. We're tired of getting involved, wanting to feel like we're good guys, and then getting kicked in the teeth for it. And because that's what the kids were hearing at home, that's what they brought to me at school."

"And you did what about this?" She sat down with the two ruby bowls of ice cream, then poured on the warmed marshmallow on top.

"God," he said, watching her.

"Now, don't get diverted. Keep talking."

He did, but with a spoon in motion. "So…I didn't see I had any choice but to volunteer for the military—because that's what I'd taught them. That you couldn't just talk. You had to show up. That even weak-kneed, gun-hating, sissy teacher types…such as myself…had the power to change things—"

"Fox. You haven't got a sissy bone in your body."

"Maybe not. But it still tends to be the stereotype for male teachers, that we're lightweight fighters, so to speak. And it bugged me, what the kids were hearing at home. Anyway, I'm just trying to explain. I felt I'd lost the right to talk to them about heroes and leaders, if I wasn't willing to stand up myself."

Phoebe put her spoon down. She was the worst sucker for sweets ever born, especially for this kind of sundae, but she suddenly knew something bad was coming. She *knew*. And she didn't prompt him when he hesitated this time because right there, right there, she changed her mind about whether he should tell her this. She wasn't a psychologist. What was she *thinking,* to be so arrogant to believe she could help?

"So…I got over there," he continued slowly. "And they put me to work, pretty much on the kinds of projects you'd expect them to assign someone like me—rebuilding schools, trying to organize the old teachers, spending time as a sort of liaison with the townspeople. I carried a gun, but I never had a reason to aim it. There were incidents. Plenty. But I wasn't really personally affected. I just did my thing, what I was getting the stripes for, what I really went there to do.…"

"Here," she said firmly. "You need cherries on that sundae. And more marshmallow—"

But when she tried to grab his bowl, he hooked her wrist instead. They weren't exactly done eating. They weren't done with dishes, either. But for some unknown reason they went outside, sat on her back steps and sipped in the crisp spring night. The dogs were chasing around the bushes, happy to be out and free. Clouds whispered a promise of rain. He dropped his jacket on her shoulders and picked up his story, his tone still as even as a tailor's hem.

"The local kids started coming around. Nothing odd about that. Kids always know when an adult honestly likes them, you know? And the kids wanted their schools back. So they started hanging with me. And I could speak some of the language, so I'd get them going. I'd teach them some English, they'd teach me some of their language. We talked about rock and roll, and games, and ideas, whatever they wanted."

His jacket was cuddled around her shoulders, when all he had to warm him was a shirt, yet she was the one whose fingertips were chilled.

"So…there was a certain morning. It was hot. Over a hundred. Sun blazing, just like every other day. I'd started work early, gotten up before anyone else—God knows why, probably because I was nuts. Anyway, I'd turned around this corner, was picking up a box of supplies, when a kid came in the alley. A boy. Not even half-grown. Big, dark eyes. Beautiful eyes. I see the way he looks, and think he must have been sleeping in that alley, so my mind's running ahead. I figure he's orphaned, and then that he might be hurt, because he's got that kind of deep, old hurt in his eyes."

Mop and Duster came flying back to flop on his feet. His feet, not hers. Damn it, they knew.

"So I start talking to him, like I always do with kids, same tone, same smile. Bring an energy bar out of my pocket, offer it to him. I'm thinking what I'm going to do if he's in as bad shape as I think he is, because I'm sure as hell not leaving him alone in that alley. I'm thinking, this is exactly what it's all about. Not the guns. Not the bull. But this. Finding a way, a real way, to give a wounded kid a life."

"Fox." There was gravel in her throat now. Gravel in her heart. It came from looking at his face, the naked sadness in his eyes.

"He had the dirty bomb under his clothes. Did something to detonate it."

"Oh my God," she whispered.

"I can't explain the rest. Why I came home so messed up, so angry. I mean, obviously it was tragic and horrible. But it's not as if I could have stopped it. I never actually saw him die, so it's not like that specific memory could be part of the nightmares. I didn't. I didn't see much of anything—I have a real vague memory of being blown against the far wall and knocked out, but that's it. I didn't know anything else for hours. But when I did wake up...I woke up angry. Beside-myself angry. Mad enough to punch walls and cuss out any-one who tried to help me—"

"Fox."

Finally he looked at her. "I haven't told my family most of that. Didn't want to. Hell, I don't honestly know where all the rage came from. But that story better be a good enough explanation for you, red, because that's all I've got. That's what happened. There's nothing else—oomph!"

Maybe he'd intended to say more, but she swooped on that man with the fury of an avenging angel. She knew he still had half-healed wounds and a half-dozen seriously sore spots. She knew it was stone chilly on the back porch steps. Most of all she knew that she'd never again intended for Fox to see her sensual side...but the damn man.

What was she supposed to do? Listen to that terrible hurt of his and do nothing? Listen to how badly he'd hurt for that child, so badly he couldn't stop hurting himself, and pretend it was just a story she was hearing that didn't affect her?

She kissed him and kept on kissing him, thinking he de-served every damn thing she could give him and then some. If he lost respect for her, then that was how the cookie crum-bled. Sex was a way to show love, to give love. To pour on love. It was only one way, but at that very second, she needed to pour five tons of love on the damn man, and she didn't have a zillion other options at her disposal. Sex was too darn handy not to use it for all it was worth.

Still kissing him, still teasing his tongue with hers, she pushed the jacket off her shoulders and then started to pull up her sweater. Both of them needed a second to suck in air, and it was that second when she yanked the sweater off her head and tossed it.

Not a great idea. Mop and Duster promptly took off with it and tore across the yard, but that was an oh-well. Fox's eyes were open at that moment. Dark and deep and confused. He opened his mouth—so she shut it again.

Headlights suddenly glowed from the neighbor's driveway—far enough away that they couldn't really see much. Or maybe they could. She didn't care. She didn't unbutton his shirt because she'd have to kill him if he caught cold because of her. She went directly for the snap on his jeans.

He needed gentle treatment, she thought. He needed tenderness.

Unfortunately, he wasn't going to get either.

At that instant she hated the kind of world that would hurt Fox that way. The kind of world where a child could die that way. It was infuriating and untenable and despairing and awful. She told him, in hot velvet kisses, in angry pressure-cooker kisses, in rubbed-in caresses and kneaded stroking. She told him, with her hands, sliding over skin, touching, owning, claiming every part of Fox she could love. She told him by closing her eyes and concentrating and emoting every ounce of love she could beg, borrow or conjure.

He hissed a swear word. She was pretty sure it was her name.

She gave him her fury…another gift she could offer through the sense of touch and sound and taste. She whispered kisses on him, closing his eyelids with the most precious touch, painting softness with more kisses down his throat. It wasn't fury the way a man would express it, but it was a torrent of feeling all the same. It was all she knew how to do. When something was this unbearable, it was all she could do. There was no fixing his wounds, so all she could try to do was share them.

She whisked more kisses down his chest, over his shirt, down to the open vee of his zipper. My. He popped up faster than a kid for candy. She couldn't make that memory disappear for him. Now, and maybe forever, she'd never make that mental picture disappear for herself, either. But she could slip her hands inside his jeans and slide that fabric down, down, down. He yelped when his bare, bony fanny connected with the cold boards of the deck.

"Is this any way to treat an invalid?" he demanded in a whisper.

"Don't try to get out of this."

"Are you out of your tree? I wouldn't want to get out of this if my life depended on it. I'd just as soon we weren't arrested for public exposure, though. At least until after."

"We might be. But my neighbors aren't kids. Don't have kids."

"Good," he murmured, and then took his turn at sweeping her under. Most of her clothes had undergone major rearranging by then. Her sweater was completely gone. One bra strap seemed to be hanging off her shoulder. Her black slacks seemed to be hanging around her hips—but only for another second or so, because once Fox got motivated, he could have given courses in inspired action.

Yet there was suddenly a moment when he slowed everything down. He threaded his hands through her hair, just looking at her in the moonlight, and then tortured them both by tuning their channel to slow, lazy motion. He scraped his bearded cheek between her breasts, polished her nipples with his tongue, took in each breast. Tenderly. Ardently. He offered a caress of tongue and teeth that pulled at every need she'd never known and made a girl-growl hiss from her throat.

"Oh, yeah, you," he murmured. "Now. Now, Phoebe…"

She was doing the seducing, darn it, but somehow…somehow he was the one strapping her legs around him, probing and then diving in, then fitting the two of them tighter than satin Velcro. Moonbeams danced in front of her closed eyes. Sunshine seemed to shine from the inside of him to the inside of her. He started the ride…a wild, wild ride on the cold porch on their dark, dark night…and something loosened in her that had never been loosened before.

It was the rage, she thought. She'd never been angry like this. That had to be it.

They both seemed to tip off the cliff at the same time. He let out a joyful yell that made her want to laugh…yet she felt the same exuberant burst of joy. Nothing was going to erase that terrible experience for him, she knew that. But for this moment—these moments—that sadness had been bearable. Love had a way of lifting and healing, she believed from the heart…which was why she simply had to offer him hers.

Eyes still closed, still breathing like a freight train, she kissed him and kissed him and kissed him. He kissed her and kissed her and kissed her. They started regaining their breath—and a cold whisk of midnight air made them both shiver…and smile at each other. A private smile that belonged to the two of them and no one else.

No one had ever smiled at her the way Fox did.

No one had ever made her feel the way Fox did.

He stroked her hair back. "You take my breath, red," he whispered.

"And you take mine."

"We're going to catch our death."

"I know. We need to go in—"

"And we will. But I just have to tell you…" He shook his head, still smiling, still looking at her with midnight-dark, loving eyes. "You're the sexiest woman I've ever known. You're my dream."

Her smile died. She froze completely—inside and out.

Nine

Fox turned the corner. Just ahead was Lockwood's restaurant, lit up brighter than the Taj Mahal. His brother Moose had never done anything halfway. You couldn't get in the restaurant door without a tie. A kid in tux parked the cars. Even on a cool spring night like this, the outside garden was decked out with teensy lights and a golden fountain. Hell, the cheapest thing on the menu was $50 a plate.

Fox parked behind the building, next to his brother's BMW. Thankfully there were back stairs, so he could sneak up to Moose's place without being seen. He was wearing old, battered jeans and a USC sweatshirt from his college years—which was held together by threads.

He hadn't played poker in over a year, and wouldn't be now if Phoebe hadn't put the idea of a night out in his brother's head. Fox had to unearth his "lucky" clothes from the depths of his closet.

And he needed some luck, he thought as he clomped up the private back stairs. Not for poker. But with Phoebe.

He thought they'd turned a milestone the other night. Making love—my God, who could deny how powerfully they came together, who they became together? Even for a man who'd never wanted love, who didn't believe he was in a position to offer love—or a life—Phoebe was forcing him to rethink everything.

If he couldn't live without her, he obviously had to find a way to kick himself in the butt, completely heal and start a real life again.

It would seem he couldn't live without her.

It would also seem that he couldn't possibly live without making love to her—preferably every night, possibly more often, for the rest of their natural lives.

Only, she'd freaked after. He mentally replayed those moments after they'd made love. Yeah, he'd told her she was the sexiest woman alive. That didn't seem like an insult, did it? I mean, for damn sure, he should have said she was the most beautiful, the most brilliant, the most wonderful woman in the world before he got to the sexy adjective. But God knew, he meant the compliment with love. He meant it with honesty. And he could have sworn Phoebe didn't need flowery packaging to tell her something straight from his heart.

Besides, he'd known she had a little thing about thinking of herself as unsexy. But that was the point. Why he'd said it. Why he'd wanted to compliment her that way. Guys prayed to find a lover who was honestly, uninhibitedly hot for them, someone who fired up for the same things he fired up for. Yet no male with a brain really thought he'd ever find that. You worked at sex just like you worked on everything else.

Except with Phoebe. She was more than his dream. Every time they touched, she felt like his missing half. He'd reached heights with her he hadn't known existed…and as far as he could tell, she had, too. Yet he'd made that comment, and suddenly she'd run inside on the excuse of their needing to warm up. Then she'd insisted his session time was up. He'd said, what the hell did that matter. She'd said, "Fergus, I thought you were only going to be here for two hours. I've got a baby scheduled to come over tonight. It's not as if I knew we were going to make love."

And that was the crux of the crisis. Not what she'd said. But that she'd called him Fergus instead of Fox.

She might as well have punched him in the stomach.

When he reached the top of the stairs at Moose's place, he knocked once, then freely opened the door. "It's just me," he called out.

But he still couldn't get his mind off Phoebe. He loved his brother, even loved to play poker, once upon a time. Just not tonight. He needed time alone. It wasn't just that he was all riled up about Phoebe, but that he needed concentrated time to think about life. A job. The serious decisions looming imminently in his future.

Still, again his mind sneaked back to Phoebe with another itchy problem. He never had gotten an answer about what happened with her ex-fiancé. That had to be a major key, he figured, because hell, if it wasn't a major key, he was in major trouble. She'd only committed to helping him for a month, and that month was up in a matter of days.

He knew, as sure as he knew he was allergic to clams, that

once that month was over, she was out of there unless he
found some way to stop her in her tracks.

"Moose? Where the hell are you?" he called out.

He assumed the poker table would be set up in the den. It
always had been. But the den was as quiet as the kitchen,
where Fox automatically opened the fridge and pulled out a
beer.

The whole upstairs apartment was bigger than it looked,
and Moose wasn't one to deprive himself of creature com-
forts. The kitchen looked like an audition for appliance
heaven, and the living room was fancied-up with a home the-
ater, set-in bar, recessed lighting and a lit-up aquarium with
exotic fish.

"Moose? Am I really the first one here?"

Past the leather and sleek technology center were a pair
of bedrooms and baths, one on either side of the hall, and then
came a long narrow sun room that Moose had always used
for an office. Now, though, Fox saw the gaming table as he
crossed the threshold. He opened his mouth to offer a greeting and instead closed it faster than a gulping fish.

Moose jerked to his feet. "Hey, Fox, didn't hear you come
in. You're a little early—"

"I know, I—"

"Fox, you know Marjorie, don't you? Marjorie White?"

"No. I don't believe I've had the pleasure." Fox stepped
forward with his hand outstretched because his mom hadn't
raised any sons who didn't know their manners. But in a single glance, he could see the gaming table had no cards on it,
no drinks, no junk food. No one else was in the room but
Moose and this woman.

And where he was dressed like a rag man and holding a

long-necked bottle of beer, she was wearing what his mom called country club clothes. Stockings. Clunks of gold here and there. Blond hair sharply styled. Subtle makeup, little black dress, expensive perfume.

"Fergus, I've heard so much about you for years."

"Well…I'm glad to meet you." He said politely, and then shot a shocked and confused look at Moose.

"I thought you two hadn't met each other before," Moose said heartily. "Marjorie doesn't teach, Fox. But she used to be married to Wild Curly Forster. Remember him? Linebacker, my class, not yours, but turned into the sharpest lawyer this side of Gold River."

"Sure," Fox said, who had never heard of the guy before.

"He died a few years ago. Car accident."

"I'm sorry," Fox said automatically.

"So you both know something about loss," Moose said firmly.

"Say what?"

Marjorie intervened with a quiet little laugh. "Your big brother is springing this surprise on you, I realize. But we don't have to make a big deal out of it, Fergus. He just thought you'd like some feminine company for a change. Let's just have a drink and talk a bit, all right?"

"Sure," Fox said, and again spared a glance at his brother. Murder was too good for him. Hell. Torture was too good for him. "I could have dressed differently, but I assumed I was coming for a poker game."

Moose slapped him on the shoulder. "Marjorie could care less how you're dressed. You two just put your feet up. Get to know each other. I put a couple DVDs in the machine, got some wine cooling. I've got to go check downstairs. We're having a hell of a gig downstairs tonight, company party for Wolcott's."

"Moose, hold up—"

"I had the boys make up a tray of finger foods, so just pull it out when either of you are hungry—"

Marjorie hadn't stopped looking at him, and now a miserable flush climbed her neck. "Fergus, I realize you weren't told about this. I never liked the idea of blind dates, either. But I'd thought, from what your brother said…I mean, it's not like I'm so hard up that I need to be set up."

"Of course you don't." Hell. Hell. Hell. Her feelings were hurt. Fox could plainly see the flush, the trembling mouth, and thought he was going to strangle his brother, and enjoy doing it. He couldn't fulfill that daydream quite that fast, though. "Marjorie, just sit down, all right? We'll talk. I really didn't mean to come across as…"

God knew how he filled out that thought. Cruel? Mean hearted? He really didn't mean to give her the impression that she was too ugly to warrant his time. She was pretty. Very pretty. Actually, she was damn near gorgeous.

She just wasn't Phoebe.

Before he could turn around, his brother had disappeared. There was nothing he could do about it—not for a few minutes. She was obviously mortified and miserable. He couldn't insult her, just because he wanted to kill his brother. Come to think of it, he'd really wanted to kill both brothers, because for damn sure, Bear had been consulted on anything Moose did.

Both of them were dirt. Turncoats. Pond scum.

He served Marjorie a glass of wine and then unearthed the platter of hors d'oeuvres, after which he listened to the entire, unabridged story of her marriage to Wild Curly Foster. Their courtship. His death. Their two children. The money he'd left her. Her evil in-laws. The trip she'd taken to Paris last year to recover from all the stress. How much she missed a man.

When the telephone rang, though, he finally had an excuse to run downstairs. The call was from the local police, asking his brother for a donation. Fox offered them a four-figure gift, but after he hung up he told Marjorie the call had been from Moose—that there was some kind of emergency downstairs; he'd check it out and promised to be right back.

Faster than lightning he charged downstairs, taking the restaurant's back door into the kitchen. He stormed past the clanging pots and steaming smells and cooks yelling at each other, past the computer service area and the maître d's. Finally he located the fink—opening wine for a crowded party in one of the restaurant's private rooms.

Moose spotted him in the doorway. Fox figured his brother must have noticed the steam coming out of his ears, because he promptly aimed his thumb toward the outside.

In the fresh, cold air of the parking lot, Fox darn near took a swing at him. "What the *hell* were you doing?"

Moose lifted his hands in a helpless gesture. "The idea was for you to rejoin life again. To get out of the bachelor house. To budge you off 'go.' To remind you of the good things in life."

"So you thought I needed fixing up with a woman!"

"I didn't say that."

"What the *hell* would you call it, then?"

"What I'd call it," Moose said calmly, "was Phoebe's idea."

"What?"

Moose slugged his hands in his pockets. "She called me two mornings ago. She knew it was my night to have you over. She assumed I'd be setting up a poker game, but she wanted to suggest a different idea. I *do* happen to know a few women, you know."

"*Phoebe* told you to set me up with a woman?" He still couldn't grasp it.

"Not set *up,* Fergus, for God's sake. She just said part of healing—part of motivating you to rejoin life again—was remembering the good things in life you used to enjoy."

"Like women?"

"Hey. I figured you'd be pissed as hell. But I guess Phoebe figured I'd be the brother who really knew women, you know? So I'd pick someone okay. And Marjorie's heard about you for a blue moon. Kind of had a crush on you from afar, or so they say—"

"I got it, I got it." There was nothing more to say, and he couldn't keep Marjorie just waiting upstairs by herself. He had to get back up there and get himself out of this. But his mind kept reeling in the information that this had been Phoebe's idea. An idea that surfaced two mornings ago…which meant it was the morning after they'd made wild, tumultuous love on her back porch.

The only conclusion he could draw was that their making love must have scared her—really scared her. Badly scared her.

But why…? He didn't have a clue.

Friday morning Phoebe was in the middle of her Baby Love wellness class when she heard a knock on the back door. She scooped up two of the babies and carried the thumb-suckers with her to answer it. Fergus grinned when he saw them.

"Got your hands full, I see." He dropped a kiss on her nose, then moved on past, carrying a toolbox—and shoes that tracked in sand, she noticed. "I just had an extra hour to spend on the waterfall, so thought I'd take advantage if you didn't have any clients in there."

"I don't. I've got a class going in the living room, but that's not a problem. How're you doing?"

"Whistling good. Couldn't be better," he assured her.

Not that Fox had ever complained, but his perky tone was distinctly unlike him. "No aches or pains at all?"

"Nothing worth mentioning. Went to the doc yesterday. He hadn't seen me in a while, claimed I looked alive for the first time in months. Believe me, that was a mighty compliment, coming from hi—"

"So," she said in her laziest tone, "did you have a good time with your brother the other night?"

He peeled off his jacket and started laying out gear, barely glancing up. "You mean Moose's night-out thing? I'll tell you the truth, red. The night did just what I think you wanted it to—jolted me good. And I can hear the babies from here—so you can go back to your class, don't worry about me."

He hunkered down on his knees with his back to her. Her mouth was still open to ask him another casual, lazy question, but somehow that was impossible now. Between the perkiness and the snappy kiss on the nose and the mysterious dark glint in his eyes, he was really acting…indecipherably different.

Had Moose set him up with that Marjorie? Had anything

happened? Was she going to chew off any more fingernails fretting about it?

Damn it. Had he kissed TOW? That Other Woman?

"Phoebe?"

When she heard one of the moms' voices, she quickly spun around and rejoined the circle in her living room. Her therapy room was huge, but still not big enough to accommodate six moms and their babies—at least when the group needed to be spread out all over the carpet. Everybody brought mats for the Baby Love class. The babies were all naked. None was older than four months.

The babies were all happier than clams. The moms were all exhausted and frazzled. Which was why she'd started the program.

"Okay, now. A relaxed baby makes for a relaxed mom…and I'm making you a promise. The more you touch your baby, the happier he'll be. We're going to do four types of massage exercises today. Playful. Enervating. Comforting. And calming. One at a time…"

She usually went around the circle, working with each baby and mom individually. And she intended to this morning, too, but after starting the group with the technique for the second exercise, she popped to her feet and strayed down the hall.

"Hey," she said cheerfully.

"Hey back," Fox said, but he didn't turn around. He'd pulled off his shirt, stripped down to old jeans and boots and gloves for the stone and mortar work. The plumbing was all done for her waterfall. So was the tile part of the pool. Really, the project was nearly done—it just happened to be at the messiest and dustiest part of the construction.

Temporarily, though, she didn't give a rat's tail about her waterfall. Even a few weeks ago, Fox would never have stripped off his shirt—no matter how hot it was—because he'd never have wanted anyone to see his scars.

They were riveting, she thought. Not pretty. But all the wounds were closed now, the swelling and discoloration completely gone. His natural complexion was more olive than pale, so even in early spring his skin had a healthy ruddiness. The breadth of his shoulders, the ripple of muscle in his forearms, spoke of how hard he'd worked to regain strength. She noticed that he hadn't shaved. The fuzz of whiskers on his chin seemed to be coming in blonder than his head hair. Mostly she noticed the strong profile, the good-looking nose and wickedly sexy eyes and…

"Is your class over?"

She jumped when Fox suddenly spoke. "No, no, I just wanted to see how you were doing. You're really moving along!"

"Yeah, the worst was the plumbing. I should be able to finish up the mortar and all this messy, smelly stuff by Saturday. So that'll also give it Sunday to dry before you've got people in here again. That sound okay to you?"

"Sounds good. So you had a really good time on your Moose's night out, huh?"

"Yeah, I'll say. Hmm. Phoebe, I think you need a different shower head than the one you picked out. One with a softer spray."

"Okay."

"You want me to pick it out, get it?"

"Yeah, whatever you think is best. Just tell me and I'll reimburse you. So…we're on for Monday, late afternoon, right?"

"Right. In fact, there's something I'd like to do with you on Monday, if you don't mind."

"Sure. What?"

"Nothing weird. But you've been pushing me to get outside, get more in the fresh air and all…and there's something I'd like to do that afternoon. Unless you object—"

"No, no, that's fine. I can do the exercises with you almost anywhere. So." She cleared her throat. "Whatever you did with Moose, you think you'll do it again?"

He lifted his head. "I hear one of those babies crying. Your class is probably wondering where you are."

She heard the baby cry, too, but still hesitated. It was one of her absolutely favorite projects, the healthy Baby Love massage group, yet still, she couldn't seem to move.

And Fergus suddenly sighed. He pushed up, from his hands on his knees and slowly walked toward her, his hands and torso covered with a thin layer of mortar dust, his jeans crusted with it. He came close enough to touch her but didn't—which was probably a good thing, because eventually she *did* have to go back to the class, and she was dressed for them in a white terry tunic and terry pants.

He came so close, though, that she could see the dark glints in his eyes. His gaze magnetized hers. She couldn't look away. That close, she could no more have looked away than stop breathing.

He said softly, "I think it's cute, Red. Your trying to set me up with other women. God knows, no one ever had the nerve to try that on me before."

She'd have answered him—except that he closed the few inches between them. His hands didn't touch her—his dusty, sweaty torso didn't touch her—but he bent down and brushed his mouth on hers. It wasn't a kiss. More…the threat of one. More…the promise of one.

"You want to know if I kissed her?" he murmured.

"No."

"You want to know if I considered—"

"No."

"Because I'll tell if you ask me. I'll be honest with you. No matter what. You'd be honest with me the same way, wouldn't you, red?"

"Yes. Of course I would," she breathed. But something about the way he'd kissed her, the way he was whispering, the way he was looking at her, had her so rattled she couldn't think straight. She was a pinch away from hiccupping from nerves. Her. The woman who could probably get a Ph.D. in laidback. "I need to go back to my class."

"I know you do."

"We'll talk later."

"Oh, yeah," he murmured. "I know you've got work today. But we're definitely going to talk again. And soon."

She stumbled back toward her class, thinking, all right, now she knew that Fergus had an ugly, evil side to him. A manipulative, wicked side. A side that turned her mind to jam and her sanity to jelly.

He talked to her as if they were lovers. Which, she guessed, they were. But she'd emotionally shut the door on believing they could make it long-term. She'd hoped—she admitted that she'd fiercely hoped—things might have turned out differently. But when he'd praised her for being "so sexy," she'd felt her heart thud like the clunk of a coin down a long, dark well.

He wanted her, she didn't doubt that. But sex, even great sex, was just no measure that he seriously valued or respected her.

Nothing had changed. She had fiercely wanted to heal Fergus—to be the one to make a difference for him—and every day, every week, she'd literally seen her efforts working. He was so, so much better, mentally, physically and emotionally. She wasn't the only one responsible for that, but Phoebe gave herself credit for playing a key role.

That was what mattered. Getting him healed. Not what she wanted. Not what she dreamed.

She stomped back into the class and blurted, "Damn it. We are going to *relax,* class!"

The moms all looked at her as if she were crazy—until someone laughed. And then she tried to laugh, too.

Ten

When Fox pulled into her driveway, Phoebe had to put up with two solid minutes of whining and begging from Mop and Duster. "I know it's Fox, you guys, but you can't go. It's not our truck. And it's raining. And you know I won't leave you alone for long. Come on, you two. Be reasonable."

The dogs had heard all that. They also knew they had the dog door open to the whole backyard, and that their dishes in the kitchen were heaped with food and fresh water. They just didn't want Phoebe to leave, and they loved being with Fergus, besides.

So did she—which was the problem. She pulled her rain jacket hood over her head to run outside. Grumbling clouds swirled, leaking more drizzle than rain for now, but warning that worse was coming. Even at four in the afternoon it was darker than winter, with moments of sudden stillness and then moments when the fresh green leaves suddenly trembled and tossed in fretful anticipation.

Lightning crackled just as she reached the door of his SUV and slammed inside.

"I was coming in to get you—"

"Well, that would have been silly. Then both of us would have gotten wet." She tossed her jacket in the backseat. The wipers and defroster had to be on because of the foggy steam, but underneath all that threat of storm, the temperature was muggy and close. She should have worn her hair up, she thought, and her long-sleeved green tee was probably going to be too warm, as well. "You still haven't told me where we're going."

For the first time, she glance at Fox, then quickly away. That was the trick, she mused. If she just didn't look at those mesmerizing eyes, that sexy narrow mouth, that *look* of him, too hard, too long, she'd be able to keep some emotional distance.

"I'm not trying to be mysterious. I just wanted to show you a place. If I told you about it first, I was afraid it'd color your reaction, so I just wanted you to see it. And I promise, it's not a long drive."

"I couldn't believe how much work you'd gotten done on the waterfall over the weekend."

"Yeah…even working around the hours you need the room, I should have it done by the end of the week."

She'd guessed that. She'd also guessed that Fergus was likely to call off their relationship completely when the project was done—partly because he was at the end of her recovery program for him as well. She had one more intensive exercise she wanted to work with him on, but Phoebe could see for herself that he was totally on the right track. Maybe he wasn't ox strong quite yet, but his shoulders and arms had regained all their muscle tone. He moved with virile, vital purpose again, energy, stamina.

He didn't need her anymore.

"You haven't mentioned having a bad headache in over a week," she said. "You're sleeping better?"

He shot her a look. "How about if we talk about how you're sleeping instead?"

Not well without him, but she could hardly say that when both of them avoided mentioning ever making love, as if saying it aloud would bite them in the butt. She said, "Okay, I get it. I won't hound you about your health for a whole two hours, okay?"

"Good. I'll hold you to it." He peered out the windshield. "Damn. I really want you to see this place. Maybe the rain'll quit."

That seemed as likely as cows flying, judging from the hissing wind and angry sky, but it wasn't as if driving were dangerous. The blacktop glistened as they took the twisting, curling road out of Gold River. Slopes turned into hills, then climbed into more mountainous terrain.

He was right. It wasn't a far drive. He turned down a gravel road that led eventually to…nothing. Where he stopped and braked, she saw a long expanse of meadow, carpeted in wildflowers, leading to a creek that splashed silver in the rain. Boulders on the other side led up to a hillside of rich, emerald-green trees.

"What do you think?"

She cocked her head curiously, unsure what he wanted her to say. Her first thought was that the wondrous place resembled the safe haven he'd described in the first exercise they'd done together...but she couldn't imagine that had any relevance to why he'd brought her here—or what he wanted her to say. "It's gorgeous."

He didn't exactly look disappointed, but something in his expression changed. Suddenly his gaze looked...careful, and his shoulders stiffened with tension. "Yeah, it's pretty. But what can you picture here? I mean, try to imagine it if it weren't raining and gloomy. If the sun were shining down on the water and the mountainside..."

"I think it's gorgeous in the rain and would be even more beautiful in the sunshine." She spoke truthfully but couldn't seem to think. He obviously wanted her to react in some way, yet she had no clue what he wanted from her.

He turned off the engine and just leaned back, staring out the window instead of at her. "I've been thinking about moving. I haven't minded being by my mom, but...I just want my own place. I rented before. That seemed the simplest choice when I didn't have the time or interest in maintaining a place of my own. But now...the idea of a home is a lot more appealing."

She could see his profile, the strong nose, the sharp eyes, but nothing in his expression gave away what he was feeling. "You feel up to making a major move?"

"I know I'm not moving at racehorse speed yet, but yeah. I'm getting there." He hesitated, as if hoping she'd comment more, but again she felt an attack of nerves.

She'd never been short of opinions, and she'd easily offered them to Fox before, but it was different now. The times they'd made love stood between them like a velvet wall. He didn't refer to them. Neither did she.

She knew how to communicate using touch. But she didn't know the words he wanted to hear.

And when she still said nothing, he filled in. "Phoebe, I wasn't trying to lead you into saying something I wanted to hear. But I was specifically thinking about building a house. Right here. I own this property, have for a while. What do you think about it for a home site?"

"I think it'd be gorgeous," she said, and then realized that seemed to be the only word that kept coming out of her mouth.

He motioned. "Probably put the kitchen there—facing east—with big glass doors leading to a deck, so a body could sit outside, eating their grapefruit, sipping their morning coffee." He waited, then went on. "Then I could see an octagonal room, glass walls—the great room facing the mountains and creek. The sun would come in there too strong, but we could fix that by using solar windows. Put the master bedroom upstairs. Make it a solid north wall, but put windows east and west, so the room would get the sunrise in the morning, the sunset in the evening."

When he paused again, she said, "It couldn't sound better, Fergus. It's a beautiful plan."

"Can you picture the house ideas?"

"You bet."

"Could you picture living in a house like that?"

She frowned. "Sure. Who couldn't? It sounds like a dream house. But…I'm not sure it'd be a good idea for you to be out this far in the woods alone, do you?"

"You've got that right. I don't want to live alone anymore." He fell completely silent then, scraping a hand through his hair and then, for a few seconds, squeezing his eyes closed.

"Damn," she murmured. "I knew something was wrong. You're getting a headache, aren't you."

"Not a headache. I just…" He opened his eyes. He suddenly looked so despairing, so frustrated. "Phoebe, I…"

"No," she said swiftly. "I can see you're hurting. Bad hurting. Don't talk. Just turn around for me, Fox. Face the side window."

"You don't understand. I wanted to—"

"No talking! I mean it!" Energy surged through her. She knew what to do when he was hurting. Anything was better than those strange moments when he kept waiting and waiting, clearly counting on her to say something and her failing to come through. Whatever that had been about mattered, but if Fox was hurting, *that* took precedence over any and everything else.

"Lean forward," she said quietly, firmly. "I told you before, I had another exercise I wanted to give you. It's like the first one we did. An exercise you can use whenever you're in pain or stressed. Not just for now but whenever you feel stressed.…"

He turned toward the driver's window—not at a perfect angle, but good enough. She knelt behind him—again not easy to do from her seat, but she could manage. Thankfully he was wearing an old, loose sweatshirt that she could push out of the way. She closed her eyes when she felt his warm, supple skin under her fingertips again. Maybe she had no oils to work with today, no soothing warm water, no props. But she had her hands, to knead into his hair, into his nape, around his temples and forehead. And she had her heart, her love, to convey through the sense of touch.

"Okay now, Fox," she whispered, "this is called the rainbow exercise. I want you to picture yourself standing at the beginning of a giant tunnel that's entirely made of color—"

"You've got to be kidding me."

She considered taking a small nip out of his shoulder, but that would be too loverlike. A headache was serious business. Healing him was no joke. "Just go along with me, okay?"

"Okay." He used that patronizing tone men used on women when they were pretending to be patient, but she didn't care. She'd won what she needed. His attention.

"Okay, now close your eyes and imagine this rainbow tunnel. Just like with a real rainbow, the first part is red. You're going to take an imaginary step inside where it's all red, Fox. I want you to feel that red, smell it, taste it, touch it. There's huge energy in that color, isn't there? Passion. Anger. High emotion…

"And then we're going to keep walking, slowly, into our rainbow. We're going to walk past the red into orange. Feel how bright and colorful and splashy the orange is? And now we're walking into yellow. All warm and healing and sunny. A happy color, yes? And you're feeling washed in that yellow. Drenched in that yellow. It's bathing you from head to toe.…"

She rubbed and stroked, his head, his temples, playing out the rainbow exercise, talking softly, soothingly. Lovingly. She could feel the knots in his neck start to ease. Feel those big strong shoulders give up some of their tension.

He was such a sucker for a head rub. Again she felt her heart surge. It was such a simple joy—knowing that she was the one who could reach him. Knowing she was the one person who could relax him, whom he could trust enough to be himself with, to let down his heart with.

"The green is so beautiful, isn't it? You can almost smell all the green things—the grass and leaves. The emerald is so alive, so full of life. But then, at last we come to blue, Fox. A deep, rich royal blue…but not dark. This is a clear blue. This is the blue color that makes you think of peace. There's no stress in this blue. No worries. No fears. Feel the blue, Fox?"

"Yup, I feel your damn blue, red."

She grinned and dropped her hands. "Okay…that's it. Just kind of wake up from this slowly. How's the headache?"

Slowly he lifted his head. Slowly he turned around. She was still crouched on her knees, waiting to see his face, to study how he was doing. The storm clouds had thundered on, but it was still raining outside—a clean, soaking downpour that hissed in the leaves and washed down the meadow. She could see his face much clearer now, and the intensity in his expression startled her.

"What did he do to you, Phoebe?"

"What?"

"The guy. The jerk you were engaged to. What did he do to you? And no ducking out this time. You promised that you'd try to be as honest with me as I was with you. You promised you'd *try*. And I told you what happened to me."

She sucked in a breath, feeling suddenly at a loss. "I didn't heal your headache? The exercise didn't work?"

"Red, you've been healing me from the day I met you. How about giving me a shot?"

"At what?"

"At helping you heal this time," he said softly, and then repeated insistently, "What did the son of a gun do to you?"

She clicked up the lock and pushed out the door. She could

have grabbed her jacket, but at the moment she just didn't care. Rain sloshed down, not hard, but too relentlessly to escape it. It slithered in her hair, matted her eyelashes.

Still she took off, hiking fast, and only moments later realized that Fox had caught up and was keeping pace beside her. He said nothing, just walked with her, getting as soaked as she was.

"Darn it, Fox! It's not something I can explain. Not to a man."

"Then forget I'm a man and just think of me as a friend."

"For Pete's sake. I *do* think of you as a friend. But I'll never forget you're a man in this life. No woman would."

"Um, I'm not sure if that's a compliment or an insult."

"It's just a statement of fact."

He said quietly, "Find a way to tell me."

Like it was that easy. And damnation, but the warm rain was squishing in her shoes now, and making her long hair feel heavier than a rope.

Besides, she didn't know where to start. "In high school…I went out with a lot of boys. Always had a good time. But also always pulled back before it went too far. I just really wanted to save it for the right guy. Girls still believe there'll be one perfect guy for them when they're in high school. Or some of us still did—"

"Okay."

"So anyway. That was the point. That I'd waited. That I thought Alan was The One. So when we got engaged…"

Fox wasn't going to waste time on euphemisms. "You did the deed. And he hurt you?"

"No."

"He scared you somehow?"

"No. Nothing like that. It went great."

"So…"

She turned on him in a fury. "If you catch cold from this walk because of me, I'm going to shoot you myself."

"Threat accepted. So go on."

She lifted her hands in a helpless gesture. "So that was the problem. That it went great. I didn't understand at first. We were engaged. Why would he be unhappy if things were going well when the lights went out? Yet from that first night, he started pulling back."

Ahead, a rabbit hopped into their path, stared at them and then hopped back under cover like any sane animal would have done.

"I guess you could say I got more adventurous. I was…blind. This whole part of life seemed…great to me. Natural. Wonderful. And I believed I loved him, so there was nothing I wasn't willing to think about or talk about or try."

"And?"

"And he was repulsed."

"Say what?"

"You heard me."

"I couldn't have," Fox said bluntly.

She sighed. There was a time she thought nothing would mortify her, but trying to talk about this did. "I could claim that we both wanted to break the engagement, but the truth is…he wanted out. It's not like he didn't want to keep sleeping with me, but he shut me off any time I brought up marriage plans after that. The better it got between the sheets, the less he trusted me. Anything I said or tried to say, somehow I ended up feeling dirty. Amoral."

"Phoebe, we may have to run through this again, because

something's wrong with my hearing. Something *has* to be wrong, because I couldn't possibly be hearing what you're telling me."

"I know you're trying to be funny. And it is, in a way. There's nothing new about the old double standard. It's been around since the beginning of time. I'm not blaming him. I'm saying there was something ingrained in him. And maybe it's ingrained in a lot of men and women. That women who are…sexy…must be of low moral character."

"That's ridiculous."

She persisted quietly, firmly. "There's a fear that a woman 'like that' won't be faithful. That if she's a great lover, she won't make a steady wife. I know, I know, we all *say* differently out loud. Alan *said* differently, too. But that's how he felt deep down. The more times we slept together, the more he pulled away, the less he trusted me, less he shared with me. Oh, for God's sake. Let's head back to the car and get out of this ridiculous rain before we both catch our death."

"Wait a minute—" He hooked her arm, not roughly, but determined to spin her around to face him.

She faced him, but she also shook her head. "I really don't want to talk anymore about this. I know what you'll say. That it's all wrong. That he was a creep. That of course a guy wants a hot woman. I mean, come on, we're not kids."

"Maybe I wasn't going to say any of that."

"Oh, yeah, you were." She lifted her face, ardently wanting to kiss him—wanting to be kissed. Actually wanting anything but to still be talking about this. "But I don't need logic or that kind of reassurance, Fox. I was just trying to tell you what happened. How it made me feel. How it affected me."

"You moved away. Gave up regular physical therapy completely. Concentrated on work with babies." He added, "I understand it took you a while to get over him. But it's been a while. You *have* to know it isn't that way with me. I can't believe you'd paint me with the same brush as that jerk."

"It's not about painting you with the same brush." She knew it'd be impossible to explain. Even to Fox. Especially to Fox. "It's about…feeling different about myself. I grew up thinking that sensuality was a good quality in myself. He…crippled that."

"You let him cripple that."

She felt stung. "Come on, that's not fair. When you knife someone where they're the most vulnerable, it's pretty hard to just…go on…as if your life hadn't been seriously changed."

Fergus touched her cheek, whispered, "You think I don't know that?"

His voice—his words—struck her with the surprise of a slap. He *did* know that. As totally unalike as their problems were, it wasn't being physically injured that had crippled Fox. It was being hit in the heart, because it was a child who'd injured him, and it was children where his whole self-image—as a man, as a leader and teacher and a role model—was founded. She'd always understood. When a child betrayed him, he felt as if he'd betrayed the child, as well.

And now she saw the parallel. When her innermost nature betrayed her, she'd felt as if she had become her own worst enemy. How do you recover when something you had believed was totally good in yourself turned out to hurt you?

Fox looked at her. Rain had soaked through his sweatshirt. It dripped from his brows, had turned his hair dark. "Is that where you want to leave it, red? You can do what I did. I gave up teaching, my life."

"I didn't give up sex. I made love with you, didn't I?"

"Yeah, you did. Which is really fascinating, when you think about it. You took on a man who was running straight to loserdom. No job. No future. Wallowing in self-pity, hiding in dark shadows. So what the hell were you doing, sleeping with me?"

"That's completely different, because you were never a loser. You were never at fault for what happened to you, even if you thought you were. None of that was who you were. You were just…hurt. You just needed time to heal."

"Maybe that's true—but you couldn't have known that. You took a chance on me. You took a huge risk with me. But now…you just want to walk away?"

She frowned, fiercely confused, sick to her stomach. Darn it, he was deliberately rattling her. "Fox, I never said that."

"Well, I want you to think about it. Because I'm not disappearing, red…unless you send me away. I'm not positive where I'm going, but I won't be hiding in the shadows anymore. I am sure of that. And I want to be sure of what you want from me."

She heard an implicit ultimatum in his voice. Not a threat. Just a fish-or-cut-bait warning—the same one she'd been waiting for weeks now. "I can't be, Fox! You don't understand!"

"Oh, yeah," he murmured. "I understand." And he turned away from her and stalked back to his car.

Eleven

Fox, standing at the stove in his mother's kitchen, pointed the royal finger at his mom. "No. Sit. You are not to help. You are supposed to sit there and drink wine and let me do the work."

"You're treating me like a dog," Georgia complained. "Sit. Stay. What kind of language is that to use with your mother?"

"Down, girl," Fox repeated when she tried to stand up again. "This is my night to cook for you, remember? You said you wanted to do this exercise of Phoebe's. That means you're supposed to put your feet up and I'm supposed to do the dinner. That's the deal."

"Something is very scary about you lately," Georgia said darkly. "At least when you were sick, I could order you around. You still didn't obey much, but you didn't give me all this lip."

"I think we always gave you a ton of lip, Mom." Before he could stop her, she'd sprinted out of the chair—carrying her wine—and was trying to see over his shoulder at the progress of the sizzling food on the stove.

"That isn't remotely related to beef Stroganoff," she announced.

"You've got that right."

"I bought all the ingredients for your favorites. Beef Stroganoff. Double blueberry pie. Waldorf sa—"

"*Sit.*"

Muttering ominous threats, Georgia retreated as far as the counter stool, but she still looked at him with nosy, suspicious eyes. Mother eyes. "What's going on," she said finally, flatly. She didn't make it a question.

Fox deserted the stove long enough to set the table—at least, his version of setting the table. He scooped up some forks and knives from the silverware drawer, added a couple of plates, then tossed some napkins on the middle of the table. He wasn't sure everything was going to be ready at the same time, but whatever. He could cook well enough not to starve. Putting together a complete dinner—especially the dinner he was trying to create tonight—was impossibly tricky.

"Fergus Lockwood, answer me," his mother said firmly.

"What's 'going on' is that this is the last dinner you have to put up with, as far as risking life and limb on something I cooked. I'm at the end of Phoebe's crazy program."

"The whole family loved the program, Fox. It made all of us feel we were doing something for you, instead of just sitting back and watching you hurt. That was awful."

"Well, I'm not admitting it out loud—at least to Phoebe—

but I've liked it, too. What can I say? I've got a helluva great family. But there's just no need for it now. I'm better. Really better." Since he was stuck talking about sticky stuff, he eased into another little matter. "It's time I moved out of the bachelor house."

"Why?" she demanded instantly. "I've loved having you so close! And the house is just sitting there. There's no reason on earth—"

"I know. You'd like all of us close. And we *are* close, but I need to get my own life back together. You know the property up on Spruce Mountain? I want to build a house up there."

"Oh. That's not too far." Georgia took a sip of wine, looking relieved. "Fergus. You put the knife on the right of the plate, not the left. That's a beautiful site up there. Still in the school district…in case a body ever wanted kids…but peaceful and quiet and all."

He motioned her to the table and started serving dishes. "So, here's the plan. You're hearing it before anyone else. I'm going to spend the year building a house up there. And next fall I'll be teaching again."

"Not this year?"

"Not this year. I'm going to coach the basketball team. Keep my hand in with the kids. Work with some of the liners." The "liners" was the term he and the principal created for kids who were on the line between failing and making it— those who could fall the wrong way if something didn't happen to pull them out of a slump. "I talked with Morgan about it two days ago. It's a done deal."

"You really are putting it back together," his mom said quietly, and then looked at the dishes in front of her. "Fox, since when did these become your favorite foods? What's this?"

"Chicken with cilantro."

"And this...well, I can see this is the holiday potato dish—"

"Yup. And dessert is a marshmallow sundae with chocolate ice cream." He added kindly, "You can have the sundae with dinner, if you want. This isn't like growing up. I won't tell if you have dessert first."

His mother lifted a fork, then put it down and just stared at him.

"What?" he asked.

"It's Phoebe, isn't it."

She didn't phrase it like a question, just like she almost never phrased things like questions when she already had a mom sense about the answers. So Fox didn't try to balk or duck.

"Yeah, it's Phoebe," he said quietly. "But don't start counting on grandchildren, Mom, because the truth is...I think I lost her."

"Oh, Fox, you—"

"No." This time his voice turned firm. Not disrespectful. Just firm. "You want the secret side of stuff, I'll give it to you. I love her. Completely. Totally. Enough so that she's the only thing in my head, the only woman I can even imagine spending my life with. But she's not seeing me the same way. I can't open a door she wants locked. And that's all I'm willing to say. Besides, this dinner is supposed to be about you. I want to hear how the bridge club's going, what's new with the neighborhood crowd, how your arthritis is."

"But, Fox, I—"

"This is the deal. No dessert if you keep asking questions." He added, "This is between her and me. There's no one else in the universe but her and me. Not as far as our private lives go."

And he couldn't talk any more about it. Not without panic climbing a sharp ladder up his spine. She hadn't even blinked when he'd talked about building the house for the two of them, much less given him even a tiny sign that she might be willing to build that home with him. And as far as the whole rotten thing her ex-fiancé had pulled on her…hell.

Fox just couldn't see how to make any move without making the situation worse. If he tried to make love to her, she'd think he wanted her for sex. If he didn't try, she'd think he'd stopped wanting her. That jerk had done a number on her from the inside, and Fox couldn't remember feeling more frustrated. That someone could twist Phoebe's sensual, loving, nurturing and, you bet sexy nature against her made him see red. Bull red. But short of finding the guy and beating him up, there was little Fox could do—and besides, that would only make him happy.

He wasn't used to feeling impotent.

In fact, he'd never felt the sensation before.

But if Phoebe needed to know how much he respected her, he'd already shown her how much he did…by reaching out to her. By revealing his most vulnerable side. By sharing his weaknesses with her the way he'd been unable and unwilling to share with anyone else.

Fox didn't just respect her in theory; he respected her with his heart. The more critical problem was Phoebe herself. The jerk had dented her self-respect. And that was something he had no way of fixing for her.

He looked down at Phoebe's cilantro chicken and the infamous holiday potatoes—the potato dish no man had been able to resist since the beginning of time. And suddenly he couldn't eat.

He had one more occasion to see her, but he doubted it would help. He'd lost her.

And he knew it.

Exhausted and frazzled, Phoebe opened the van door and let Mop and Duster leap up on the seat. They faced the window and determinedly ignored her.

"Look, guys. Everybody has to have shots. The vet loves you. The nurse loves you. You hurt their feelings when you treat them like they were torturers, did you ever think of that?"

Neither pup bothered to turn around. She'd pay all day for taking them to the vet. Probably have to feed them steak. Take them for extra walks. Suck up for hours. She knew what to expect. They'd been through this before.

Phoebe drove straight home, relieved it was Saturday, because she'd lost all her usual energy. She didn't want to work, didn't want to see people, didn't want to do anything. As soon as she got home, she was inclined to lock all the doors and mope in peace with the dogs.

At the base of her driveway, she stopped at the mailbox, picked up three bills, five catalogs and a reminder that she needed to renew her physical therapist's license this coming fall. She was still shuffling through envelopes when she glanced up and realized that there was already a vehicle in her driveway. A white RX 330.

Fox's car.

The pups noticed it at the same time she did and, turncoats that they were, promptly commenced a barking frenzy until she braked and let them out. They zoomed for the door, Mop quivering with excitement, Duster's tail swishing the ground in equally ardent fervor. "What is it about him," Phoebe muttered, but it was a silly question, when she already knew what it was about Fox that inspired the female of the species to fall totally and irrevocably in love.

She shouldn't have been that surprised he was here, because she'd given him a house key weeks before. It just made sense. He tried to work on the waterfall when she didn't have clients and he wasn't in her way. Usually, though, he didn't show up early on Saturday mornings, because she often had neighbors over...and, besides, this Saturday she'd just thought he wouldn't come.

He hadn't called or been around since their walk in the rain.

She knew she was to blame, which ached all the more—because she'd only told him the truth. She couldn't seem to get past what Alan had done to her—how to get past the whole feeling that she wasn't...good. That the sensual and sexual part of her nature was a flaw instead of something good and natural. The thing was, when a girl got down and naked with a man and then he crushed her for it, it did something to her spirit. Her heart. Her self-respect.

And Phoebe believed she'd had no choice but to be frank with Fox...until she'd gotten home that day, walked into her bedroom, peeled down for a shower and started crying her eyes out.

Maybe she'd told him the truth...but she suddenly realized there were other truths. She kept remembering what he'd said at the house site—how he wanted to build a deck off the kitchen, a place to sit outside, eat grapefruit in the morning....

Grapefruit. Her vice, not his. Her goofy favorite food, no
his. He'd been talking about living in that house with he.
Building that house for *them*.

And until that grapefruit word poked in her mind an
stabbed her sharply, she just hadn't realized that Fox wa
thinking about her seriously. Not as a lover. But as a wife. No
as a red-hot mama when he needed healing.

But as the kind of woman he might be willing to share
grapefruit with when they first got up in the morning.

Now she took a gulping huge breath. From the sound o
the pups barking, they'd already located Fergus in the bac
room. She peeled off her fleece jacket, stashed her bag an
mail on the kitchen counter, pushed off her shoes and trie
to think how to handle seeing him, greeting him.

No magical or brilliant ideas occurred. She shook her hai
loose, took a big breath and then walked to the doorway o
her therapy room—then stopped, still.

The waterfall was done. Or it sure looked that way.

Fox was crouched down with the dogs, making a fuss, rub
bing tummies and baby talking to them. There was still
mountain of trash and debris that he'd obviously just starte
to clean up, but the waterfall itself took her breath away.

It was her dream. The backdrop wall and sides were mor
tared in river stone. There were steps, as if you were in na
ture and really walking from shallow water into a deepe
pool before you stepped under the waterfall. The tall window
above had the effect of skylights. You could lie in the pool
look up and see sunlight or stars, be secluded from the res
of the massage room environment. Lighting had been buil
into the lower pool. The outside steps had places to set fern
and plants.

"Oh, Fox," she whispered hopelessly. "It's so, so perfect."

He spun around at the sound of her voice and immediately stood up. If the light hadn't been straight behind him, she might have perceived his expression, but as it was, she caught his dusty knees, his rough-brushed hair, but his eyes were in shadow. "You're here just in time."

"In time for what?" she asked, and then shook her head for asking such a silly question. "Obviously in time to help clean up—"

"No. That'll wait. I need a victim, an experimentee. Translate that to mean 'sucker.' Your waterfall's done, ready to test. I know it *works*, but I don't want to put everything away until I'm positive we've got it all the way you want—height of the hidden shower head, water pressure, water temperature and all that stuff. I don't think we'll have to make any major plumbing adjustments—please God—but I still want to test the details."

"Sure. What do you want me to do?"

"Just use it the way you'd use it. Close the drain. Turn it on. Fill up the pool the way you would if you were using it with a client. Just make sure everything's the way you expected, then we'll drain it and call it quits. I'll keep cleaning up in the meantime."

Something inside her froze for the oddest second. It was as if her heart understood she had a choice. One choice. Right then. A choice, a chance, that would disappear if she didn't take it.

Fox turned away again. Flanked by the dogs, who seemed to think he desperately wanted their company constantly, he started stacking spare parts, gathering trash, putting away tools. The whole time he kept up a conversation. "Now, you're used to using oils in your work, right? You can't in this. You'll need your clients to take a 'clean' shower to get the oils off before they soak in the waterfall tub, or it'll be too slippery."

"I hear you," she said, as she pulled off her shirt. Fox didn't glance back, just kept working.

"And then, I've been thinking about a way you could rig up a sling for babies. I assume that's part of what you want to do, right? Use it for the little ones?"

"I had in mind using it for all ages. But when I'm working with babies, part of my idea was having their moms in there with them. So both of them could relax at the same time," she said, as she peeled off her jeans and socks.

"Yeah, I figured that. So this sling idea…it'd be like a little hammock. Soft. But water flowing in and around it. Obviously you wouldn't leave a baby alone in it, but it would be a way for a small child to feel the flow of water without it overwhelming him." A couple of hammers and crowbars made a heck of a racket when he piled them in one long metal container.

Slowly, her stomach starting to curl, she unsnapped her navy lace bra and let it fall. Then walked barefoot into the new waterfall tub and turned on the faucets. "That sounds ideal for the babies," she said. She stood there, not getting wet yet, just lifted her hand to the spray until she had the water temperature nice and warm.

She wasn't completely naked yet. She was still wearing her favorite thong—the navy satin one, with the red, white and blue flag in the triangle. They weren't the underpants of a shy, retiring girl. They weren't underwear for a woman who wasn't inherently in-your-face sexy. Which, of course, was why Phoebe had always worn the kind of clothing where no one could see them.

"Okay…well, while you're letting the pool fill up, I'm going to start making a bunch of trips out to the truck. It's going to take me quite a—" He turned around. Saw her.

Dropped a crowbar. Then a hammer.

While he was speechless, which she suspected wouldn't last long, she stepped under the waterfall spray. "You got the water pressure perfect," she called out.

He dropped the whole damn toolbox.

She lifted her face to the pelting spray, feeling the water gush and rush and slink down her face, her throat, her body. Her hair went from a tidily brushed mass into a heavy, thick, water-soaked rope in seconds. She closed her eyes, trying not to feel how hard her pulse was thudding, her badly her tummy was twisting, how scared she was.

When it came down to it…this was how she used to feel when she was younger. About herself. About life. It would never have occurred to her that it wasn't a joyful thing to enjoy the feel and the smell of fresh warm water on her bare skin, to love the explosion of her senses. To want to be this free—for a lover. With a lover. Open. Open in her heart, open in her mind, open to wherever the senses could take them both.

It had been gone—that freedom, that feeling—for a while now. And it wasn't totally back. Phoebe wasn't positive she'd ever totally get it back…but she knew, positively, that's how she wanted to be for Fox. With Fox. With the man she loved.

"And you've got the temperature perfect," she called out, and in that second, when she was blinking water out of her eyes, she almost jumped to the ceiling…because there was Fox.

Right there. His eyes inches from her eyes. His mouth inches from her mouth. He was still wearing all his clothes, except for his boots. His work socks already looked heavier than cement, and the rest of his work clothes were molding to his body faster than glue.

"Most of us," she said tactfully, "remove our clothes before taking a shower."

"Don't you mess with me, red."

She sobered, softened. "I'm not messing with you."

"This is a pretty brazen, bawdy thing for you to do. Stripping in front of me. Getting naked in front of me."

"Yeah, I know," she said regretfully.

"You could give a guy ideas. Bad ideas. Ideas like…that you know how delectably beautiful that body of yours is. Like…that you want me to notice how delectably beautiful that body of yours is—"

"Fox?"

"What?"

"This is what you're going to be stuck with. A brazen, bawdy woman. Who likes to get naked. For her lover. Only for her lover. No one else."

"Oh, I hope so," he whispered, and then leaned down and took her mouth. It was a kiss that started out hard and firm and just got more tenacious. The pelting warm water couldn't compete with this steam.

Her Fox, her crazy wonderful Fox, seemed to forget that he was standing there in all his clothes. He framed her face in his hands and kissed her and kept on kissing her, closed-eye kisses, tongue kisses, silver kisses, come-on kisses, claiming kisses.

She was still feeling nervous and worried. But maybe not

quite as worried and nervous as she started out, because a competitive streak seemed to kick in.

She could do kisses.

In fact, she could do downright fabulous kisses. For the right man. And Fox was so totally the right man.

She made him suffer through an intensive repertoire. She tried whisper-soft kisses and ardent, take-me kisses. Wooing kisses and shy, silky kisses. Kisses involving tongues and teeth, and kisses that barely touched, only hinted at what the future might hold. Could hold. If he was a very, very good boy.

"Phoebe?" he gasped in a breath.

She took the chance to gasp in some air, too. "What?"

"We're drowning."

"That's not the serious problem, Fox. You want to know the serious problem?"

"Yeah, I do."

"You have all your clothes on. And that really is a problem that needs fixing immediately."

"I'll help," he assured her, and there was a grin. A dark, intimate, wicked, pure, guy grin. The memory burst in her mind of how she'd first seen Fergus...so low, so sad, so unreachably angry and lost. It wasn't her fault that that grin inspired her to huge, vast heights of risk. Getting wet clothes off a guy was no easy task...but she was up for it.

He was also definitely up for it, in every sense—particularly as she followed each loosened button with a kiss everywhere and anywhere she discovered bare skin. By the time she'd battled four shirt buttons, he was ripping off his belt, trying to tear off his jeans.

By then, the water in the pool had filled to knee height.

Unfortunately, everything suddenly went kaflooey. His jeans were too soggy, too stuck to him, to pull off the rest of the way. He tried. She tried. They bumped heads and staggered back, and both ended up sitting in the water with the waterfall exuberantly splashing water on both of them, and Fox, laughing, roared out, "Damnation. I need *help!*"

"You think I'm not trying?" She'd started helplessly laughing, too, and between his sitting and bracing and her pulling, they managed to win the war with his pants.

"You're not supposed to have *fun* when you're this desperate," he grumped.

But his laughing and grumping was what sealed his fate, she thought. And hers. Because the more they battled his pants, the more they laughed, the more they loved…the more she knew it was going to be all right with Fox. To be herself. Always. That this was the one man she could be with.

Fear melted away, not all at once, but in flashes of searing sensation…like when his teeth scraped the hollow of her shoulder. Like when his hands slid down her ribs, around her spine, onto her fanny, where he clenched his hands and drew her tight and hard against him. When she reached back to turn off the water—before the pool overflowed all over kingdom come—he could barely seem to give her that spare second before he reached for her again, too impatient and hungry to wait.

"I love you, red. Not just want you. I *love* you. Now. Tomorrow."

"And I love you back," she said fiercely.

"I mean *love*. And you can take it to the bank, we're going to love the sex. It's going to be hot and wild and inventive for a long time."

"You think?"

"I think. Because I trust you." He lifted his head for just that moment, so she could see his eyes. So he could see hers.

And then he sank inside her, wrapping her legs tightly around his waist. Sunlight blazed through the skylight, shining gold on his shoulders, on his forehead. The water glistened on his skin like magic crystals. Night would have offered more concealment, more privacy, but this, Phoebe thought—she *knew*—was how she wanted to be with him. Naked, physically and emotionally. Her soul as bared as his.

Her risks as great as his.

"Take me," she whispered. "Higher. Hotter. Every which way, my love."

"No," he whispered. "You take me. All the way."

Needs spiraled the more she clung to him. Tension built the more he teased and stroked. She twisted in the water, claiming him. He swirled her beneath him, claiming her. The doorbell rang. The dogs barked. Her cell phone beeped. He sank under the water once, stealing a kiss that way…but by then their playfulness had turned serious. Heart serious. Future serious.

For so long, Phoebe had felt unsure of herself. Not as a person. Not as a worker. But as a woman.

Fox didn't give her that confidence back. But for him, she found that steel-strong well inside of the woman she wanted to be. The woman she could be. With a man who challenged her to reach for it all.

When it was over, he sank back against the tile, gasping, pulling her with him, both semi-floating in the warm water until they caught their breath. His cheek nuzzled her cheek. "Are you going to kill me if I tell you you're the most beautiful woman alive?"

"No."

"What if I told you you're the brightest, the most creative, the most generous and wonderful woman in the universe?"

"I guess I'll survive if you told me that, too." She sighed, knowing where his teasing was leading up to, because she knew him so well. "Go ahead. It's okay. You can say it."

"I don't want to tick you off. Especially right before I discuss something serious with you."

"You won't tick me off."

And out it came. "You're the sexiest woman in the galaxy, red. You're my dream of a mate. You make me proud to be a man, because of how you respond to me. With me."

"All right," she said warningly. "Now you've done it—"

When she reached for him, determined to mete out the punishment he deserved—and earned—he stopped her. "*Wait,* wait. I really do need to ask you something serious first. And before that, there's something I have to see."

"What?"

He insisted they get out of the water, and then he chased her upstairs. His excuse was that they were both more wrinkled than prunes and needed to get out of the water, but she figured out pretty quickly that he'd built up a humorous curiosity about her bedroom.

In the upstairs bathroom, they toweled off and then sprinted for her bed, diving under her down comforter until they warmed up again. Then he leaned back against the pillows, pulling her onto his chest, while he looked around.

"That's what I couldn't wait to find out. What color your bedroom would be, because of all the colors you used downstairs." He shook his head in surprise.

"I didn't have a lot of money to decorate when I moved

here. And what money I did have, I needed to use on the downstairs where clients could see—"

"And that's why you chose white up here?"

She looked around at the familiar furnishings—the down comforter and rug, the painted dresser and giant wicker rocker and antique bench. "I didn't want virgin white," she said honestly. "Or bridal white. But when I came here, I kind of wanted blank-slate white. Because that's what I was trying to do when I moved here. Start over. Figure out who I was all over again. Start with a blank slate, if I could."

He scooched down, so they were face-to-face on the same pillow. "Would you consider putting a marriage date down on that slate, red?"

Her heart stopped, then came damn close to bursting.

"Don't say no," he insisted. "Hear me out. I want to build that home for us. For us—and for any kids we might want to add along the way. I know I'm unemployed and don't look like such a great bet right now. But I've got a good slug of savings put away. And I'll start some real-work teaching next fall."

Damn the man, but if he didn't force her to kiss him again. Softly. On the temple and cheek and chin. She had to kiss him. Softly. On the temple and cheek. "I'm glad," she whispered.

"You knew I'd go back to teaching."

"I know you adore kids. But I didn't know if you'd realized you were healing."

"I wasn't. Until I met you. You healed me, Phoebe. But it scared the hell out of me when I realized you were hurting, too. And I had no idea how to be the healer for you."

"Fox."

"What?"

"Love's what heals." Since she'd kissed his one cheek, she had to kiss the other. Beneath the covers, he was starting to perk up again. Oh, this man was going to be trouble for a long, long time. "Love's what's always going to heal," she whispered.

"Does that mean—"

"It means, yes, I love you. From my heart. With my heart."

"And does it mean—"

"Yes. Yes. Yes."

He stopped asking questions. That seemed to cover it all.

* * * * *

THE SECRET DIARY

**A new drama unfolds for six
of the state's wealthiest bachelors.**

This newest installment continues with

STRICTLY CONFIDENTIAL ATTRACTION

by Brenda Jackson

(Silhouette Desire #1677)

How can you keep a secret when you're
living in close quarters? Alison Lind vowed
never to reveal her feelings for her boss,
Mark Hartman. But that was before she
started filling in as nanny to his niece
and sleeping just down the hall....

*Available September 2005
at your favorite retail outlet.*

COMING NEXT MONTH

#1675 CONDITION OF MARRIAGE—Emilie Rose
Dynasties: The Ashtons
Abandoned by her lover, pregnant Mercedes Ashton turned to her good friend
Jared Maxwell for help. Jared offered her a marriage of convenience…that
soon flared into unexpected passion. But when the father of Mercedes's
unborn child returned, would her bond with Jared be enough to keep their
marriage together?

#1676 TANNER TIES—Peggy Moreland
The Tanners of Texas
Lauren Tanner was determined to get her life back on track…without the
assistance of her estranged family. When she hired quiet Luke Jordan, she
had no idea the scarred handyman was tied to the Tanners and prepared to use
any method necessary—even seduction—to bring Lauren back into the fold.

**#1677 STRICTLY CONFIDENTIAL ATTRACTION—
Brenda Jackson**
Texas Cattleman's Club: The Secret Diary
Although rancher Mark Hartman's relationship with his attractive secretary,
Alison Lind, had always been strictly professional, it changed when he was
forced to enlist her aid in caring for his infant niece. Now their business
arrangement was venturing into personal—and potentially dangerous—
territory….

#1678 APACHE NIGHTS—Sheri WhiteFeather
Their attraction was undeniable. But neither police detective Joyce Riggs nor
skirting-the-edge-of-the-law Apache Kyle Prescott believed there could be
anything more than passion between them. They decided the answer to their
dilemma was a no-strings affair. That was their first mistake.

#1679 REFLECTED PLEASURES—Linda Conrad
The Gypsy Inheritance
Fashion model Merrill Davis-Ross wanted out of the spotlight and had
reinvented herself as the new plain-Jane assistant of billionaire Texan
Tyson Steele. But her mission to leave her past behind was challenged
when Tyson dared to look beyond Merrill's facade to find the real woman
underneath.

#1680 THE RICH STRANGER—Bronwyn Jameson
Princes of the Outback
When fate stranded Australian playboy Rafe Carlisle on her cattle station,
usually wary Cat McConnell knew she'd never met anyone like this rich
stranger. Because his wild and winning ways tempted her to say yes to night
after night of passion, to a temporary marriage—and even to having his baby!